THE DAUGHTERS: ZOE

A struggle of life and faith

by

Sue White

xulon PRESS

The Daughters: Zoe
A struggle of life and faith
by Sue White

Printed in the United States of America

ISBN 9781619046009

www.xulonpress.com

PROLOGUE

~ *May of 1872* ~

Poet Walt Whitman, who served as a medical assistant during the War Between the States, said *Future years will never know the seething hell and the black infernal background, the countless minor scenes and interior of the secession war; and it is best that they should not. The real war will never get in the books.*

All in all, life was settling down after almost seven years of the awful, unbelievable holocaust that scourged the nation. The country was back where it had started, five years earlier. Actually, in many ways, it was less than it had been five years earlier. The north and south were occupying the same ground, no borders had changed. However, the biggest change came in the fact that 600,000 men and women were no longer citizens of this great country. They were gone. They would not raise families. They would not celebrate holidays with loved ones. They were no longer among the living.

No one who had survived those tragic years was the same. Really, the only victor in the country was *The Declaration of Independence*. "That all men are created equal," was the somewhat challenging theme that drove the nation to its knees.

A peek into the lives of the Smallwood, Wilson and the Casey families finds change with both heartache and celebration. Margie and Jason have been married for over five years. Dr. Martin Smallwood, Margie's brother, is serving as a Colonel and a surgeon in the Army of the United States. He and Rose Butler had married in January of 1865. Their first child was born in the fall of that year. Rose, Martin and Baby Patrick are living in officers' quarters at West Point Military Academy in New York State. Martin is serving as the Commander's Surgeon at West Point.

The rest of the family is still living in the general area of Tampico, Indiana. Casey's Emporium had grown to a wonderful general store and is managing in the postwar era. The children are in various stages of maturing. Trey, the oldest of the five Casey children, is married and proving to be a great help to his father with the business. Jeremy, also working in the family business, is seriously courting a nice young lady from a neighboring county. Joshua is attending the University of Indiana working on an undergraduate degree in Philosophy and Religion. Jacob is preparing to go away to college and the family is secretly grieving thinking about being without Jacob's presence among them. Abby is ten years old going on twenty. She keeps everyone engaged as her lively outlook on life is so charming.

As for Emma, Clayton and Zoe, Margie's children, life is a mishmash of excitement and opportunity. Emma is finishing her schooling and looking forward to becoming a teacher's apprentice some place near home. Clayton, who was the most withdrawn of the all the children really just spends his time *hanging around*. Zoe, well, that's a horse of a different color. Much like the references to the final scenes of the Book of Revelation, you never knew who, what or how Zoe would appear. She might remind you of the fiery red horse or one of the other three horses: dappled grey, black, or white. That is - she might appear foreboding, head-strong or as innocent as the driven snow.

There is one more addition to the five Casey siblings and the three Wilson children. That would be Barton Smallwood Casey, a bouncing baby boy who was born to Margie and Jason just after Christmas, 1867. He is as busy as his name sake, Uncle Barton Smallwood, had been. Well into his second year he keeps everybody hopping. The standard family questions are, "Where is Barton? And, what is he into now?"

Margie's father, George Smallwood, has finally returned from the war to rejoin his beloved Margie. He had received a very disturbing letter while he was convalescing in a Union Army camp. George had been traveling for several years throughout the conflict as a War Correspondent. After Margie's mother, Emma, died he just didn't have the will to go on. Hiding among the battles and the atrocities of war kept him more than occupied. It kept him busy just *staying alive.* He didn't have time to think and didn't want that time.

When he found Margie he was very surprised that she had remarried after Bill Wilson's tragic death. The short version would be - he soon learned to respect and appreciate Jason Casey. Everyone who knew Jason loved and respected him. As a Christian man, and a loving husband and father, Jason Casey is what the world needs more of.

What George hadn't counted on was meeting Renee Butler. Renee and Margie had been neighbors back in Ewing County. Actually, Renee was more than a neighbor to Margie. Renee had put herself aside to step in and help Margie and the children through their devastating time of Bill's tragic death.

Several years later, Renee and her daughter, Rose, had come to Tampico, at Margie and Jason's invitation. The war had landed in the big middle of where she and Rose were living just over the Kentucky-Indiana border. Renee was a natural healer and had been a doctor's assistant for the past ten years. Neither George nor Renee ever expected to find love again, but really . . . love found them. They married and were extremely happy living in Tampico. George worked with Jason at the Emporium and Renee was Doctor Cumming's able assistant.

The war to end all wars had made huge changes in the lives of all who survived it. Time had healed some losses, and families had picked up the pieces and bravely carried on to meet the future through their faith in God .They believed God would lead them on.

~ 1 ~

"To those who use well what they are given, even more will be given, and they will have abundance. But from those who do nothing, even what they have will be taken away."
Matthew 25:29

M argie had been down to Casey's Emporium. Jason loved having her come as often as she could. She always had the best ideas for displaying merchandise, especially things that women buy. Today she had arranged a display of new fabric just in from the east coast. Adding, accessories: shoes, belts, handbags, lovely tortoise shell combs and a few of the latest *chapeaus*, she had completed the lovely display. She could have put an outfit together for herself. Jason wouldn't mind. She could *confiscate* any of the store's goods anytime she wanted. But, with eight children still dependent on Jason and her, she would rather *make do*.

She had just gotten home and was checking on everybody when she realized that Zoe was missing - - again. She hadn't come home from school. They usually found her sulking in the woods behind the house. When Zoe didn't get her way everyone suffered. She and Clayton had just turned thirteen and the hormones had set in. Actually, she was moody enough without the complications of female emotions which added to the process of growing up. Clayton stayed out of her way. In fact, almost everybody did. Zoe was a very gifted young lady. She could sing like a lark, play the piano and the violin, and drama . . . well, drama was not a strong enough word to refer to or describe Zoe's antics.

Jacob has just come home from school. He had finished his final exams that day and was hoping to celebrate. Instead, he was met at the door with, "Jacob, Honey, would you mind seeing if you can locate Zoe? She should have been home from school by now. I expect she has run off to the woods again."

Mother Margie had requested his services. What was new? Jacob's thoughts chased his future with the recurring comfort . . . *Oh, how glad I will be to get away from this mad house. Am I the only one with any sense at all?* Jacob loved his family. You really had to love them to abide them. There were seven still at home, well, really eight but Joshua was off at school. Jacob was next to the oldest left to cope with all the younger ones. Poor Emma, she would be left as the major domo when he left for college. Jeremy was still at home, but he was no help. Jacob was betting on Emma, solid, safe, loving Emma. They had grown up together and were closer than any full-blooded brother and sister could be.

Emma was only three and a half when her mother had married Jacob's father. Jason was left a widower with five children when his dear wife, Amanda, died giving birth. Jacob often thought of his mother. He had been the baby for over seven years when his baby sister, Abby, was born. Jacob had three older brothers, Trey, Jeremy and Joshua. Emma and her siblings, the twins, Clayton and Zoe, had come to join their family when he was almost eight.

Back to reality. "Jacob, did you hear me? Would you please go look for Zoe," Margie had interrupted his reverie. He had to go find Zoe. Dear Zoe, what a "mess" she was. *How did that happen?* He thought. *She had the same mother and father as Emma, but she was nothing like them or anyone else he had ever met.*

It didn't take him long to get to the place where he usually found her. She had a special grove of trees where a small rippling creek made its way through the rocks and grass. There was a huge flat rock that made a wonderful place to sit and watch the water run over the rocks or even lie down in the soft grass and let the sun stream through the trees to bathe your face with a soft glow.

But, she wasn't there! *Where could she be?* Jacob checked some other spots that he knew about. However, Zoe wasn't to be found. He had been searching for over an hour, and he was beginning to get worried. *Maybe I should go back to the house? I'll bet she came home - - only God knows where she's been or what she's been doing.*

Jacob reviewed the events of the past several weeks. He was aware that Zoe was acting out in school. Actually, he wasn't a student any longer. He had continued through the year as a Teacher's Helper. He was studying with Miss Bennett to get ahead on his entrance exams for college. He was a great help in the classroom. There were twelve grades and only three teachers. Miss Bennett was the Supervising Teacher and taught the older young people.

I should have said something to Mother about Zoe. Zoe had been on a "tear" flirting and carrying on with the Jenkins boy. He was three years older than Zoe and was always bothering the girls. He seemed particularly attracted to Zoe. The worst part, she wasn't "bothered." She was delighted at the attention. *Lord, has she done something crazy?*

Margie was in the kitchen helping Tammy get supper started. Dear Tammy, what would the Casey/Wilson clan have done without her all these years? Tammy had come to live with the Casey's before Jacob was born. She had then just turned sixteen. Her mother had died giving her birth and leaving her an orphan. She didn't have a father; at least no one knew who her father might be. People called those babies *Wood's Colts*. It was as though they just wandered out of the woods one day. Now, she was in her mid-thirties and had been perfectly happy to be a part of such a fine family. Her cooking and baking skills were faultless, but her daily care for the children had truly been a godsend.

Jacob found Margie and as she looked up from kneading dough, she registered a look of concern, "Jacob, you found her didn't you?"

"No, ma'am, I didn't. I've been looking for over an hour. I'm really worried and I, uhhhh, need to talk to you about something."

"What do you mean, Jacob, *something what*?" Margie had quit kneading the dough and reached for a tea towel to wipe the flour from her hands. She was turning her full attention to Jacob.

"Well, Zoe has been acting strange at school. I know I should have said something, but I didn't want to get her in trouble."

"What do you mean, strange, Jacob?"

"I mean . . . uhhhh, she's late to class. She doesn't have her homework done, and she's been hanging around with Adam Jenkins."

"Adam Jenkins! He's much older than Zoe. Jacob, what are you saying?"

"I don't know. I don't know what I'm saying. I'm just worried."

"Jacob, hitch up the buggy – I have to go find Jason."

The dough could wait – in fact, the whole world was put on hold. Where was that girl? And what was she doing? Margie was trying to be calm, but it wasn't working.

~ 2 ~

"Let those who are wise understand these things. Let those with discernment listen carefully. The paths of the LORD are true right. The righteous people live by walking in them."
Hosea 14:9

Jason wasn't at the store. He had gone out on a delivery himself. Margie took off from the store much faster than she should have. Her dear "Sugar," the best little "cart pony" in the world was not as young as he had once been. Margie's trusty friend had served her valiantly over the past ten years. He responded easily and faithfully to her familiar touch. She jumped up into the little buggy and jerked the reins to hurry off. As she backed Sugar away from the hitching post in front of the store, Margie didn't see the huge wagon right behind her. It was loaded down with logs. Her mind wasn't on what she was doing. All she could think about was Zoe.

The huge wagon was being pulled by a double team of mules. It was moving at a reasonable rate of speed, but the driver could not miss her. The lead mules couldn't avoid the collision and ran over the little buggy spilling Margie into the road with the buggy on top of her. Bringing the heavy wagon to a halt was a Herculean feat. When it was finally stopped two of the mules had tromped over the buggy. Sugar wasn't in the direct path the mules had to take, but the scene was indeed serious with pony, buggy and a team of four mules thrown into total panic. Not to mention the buggy's passenger. The noise was enough to scare everyone within a block of the scene.

The wagon driver's assistant bounded from the wagon to grab the mules' halters to try and still them. Margie lay bleeding and broken in the middle of the mess. People were gathering and several had rushed to her aid. Lifting the pieces of the buggy off of her battered body, it was obvious that she was injured, just how badly she was injured remained to be seen.

Jason had pulled into the alley in back of the store. He heard the commotion as he turned the corner from the road. Of course, having no idea that Margie was involved, he walked into the back of the store and heard someone shout, "It's Mrs. Casey. She's hurt pretty bad!"

Surely not! Jason ran for the front of the store and was through the crowd just as Doctor Cummings and Renee arrived. "Move away, folks, move away!" One of the bystanders was giving directions.

Renee got to Margie before the doctor or Jason stepped into the circle. "Margie, Margie, honey, it's me Renee. We're here. You're gonna be all right. Just take it easy. Try not to move. Let us take care of you."

"Move aside, people," Dr. Cummings giving orders now. "We need some breathing room here. The excitement's over. Just step back."

Jason was right behind him, "Margie, Margie, oh, God . . ." his voice trailing off.

He was trying to take in the whole scene. "What happened?" Jason was kneeling at Margie's side by then. Renee was assisting the doctor as he began to examine and assess the injuries.

"She's pretty bad, Jason," Doctor Cummings was talking under his breath as he looked at Renee with that "doctor – nurse" look that says. *Stay calm. Do your best. We need lots of skill here.*

"Someone bring the stretcher from my office. Don't move, Margie, you have a broken leg and a broken arm. Just be still. You'll be fine. We're going to take care of you."

Margie's eyes opened, and she seemed to be trying to look around her. She saw Jason and half moaned, half speaking, "Oh, Jason, I'm so sorry . . . I can't find Zoe. She's gone, Jason . . . can't find her . . ." With that huge effort to deliver her message, Margie mercifully fainted.

Meanwhile, waiting at the house to see what the next move was to locate the lost Zoe, Jacob was sick with worry about her. He was beginning to feel responsible. He decided the best thing to do was resume the hunt. He saddled up and headed for the store, and when the mess in front of the store came into view he realized that the pile of rubble was Margie's little buggy. He raced on down the street and saw Trey heading off, leading Sugar. The poor beast was limping slightly – but didn't look too worse for wear.

"Trey, Trey, hold up! What's going on? Where's Margie? Where's Dad?"

"Oh, Lordy, Jacob, it's a mess. They've taken her over to the doctor's office. She backed Sugar into on oncoming log wagon. It's a wonder she wasn't killed. Dad is with her."

"Do you know why she came down here, Trey?"

"No, do you?"

"Yes! She was coming to find Dad. Zoe's missing. I've been looking for her for the past hour and a half. She didn't come home from school."

"She isn't home yet?"

"No, and I told Margie that I had seen her hanging around with Adam Jenkins."

"Not good, Brother, not good - - that girl!"

"Oh, God, Trey, is . . . Margie gonna' live?"

"Yes, we have to believe that. Some of the folks who were here when it happened said she was hurt pretty bad. They overheard Doctor Cummings say her leg and arm were broken. They took her to his office. I haven't heard anything else."

"Well, I'm gonna' go and see what's happening there at the doc's office. I'll be able to tell Dad about Zoe."

"Okay, I'll be there as soon as I can get Sugar to the livery and see what we can do for him."

~ 3 ~

"My child, listen to what I say, and treasure my commands. Tune your ears to wisdom, and concentrate on understanding. Cry out for insight, and ask for understanding. Search for them as you would search for silver; seek them like hidden treasures. Then you will understand what it means to fear the LORD, and you will gain the knowledge of God."
Proverbs 2:1-5

Indeed it would be Margie's fondest hope that Zoe would listen to her parents and "tune her ears to wisdom." Zoe pretty much did as she pleased. Thirteen going on twenty, would describe Zoe's attitude toward life. She had always behaved as though she was old enough, wise enough and entitled to do whatever she wanted to do. This latest "die-doe," was the last straw. Of course, Zoe hadn't been located yet. Perhaps everyone was jumping to conclusions. *Oh, please God let it all be okay.* Trey prayed as he walked.

Trey knew Adam Jenkins the way boys know other boys. How many times had he heard Margie tell them all – "All you have is your good reputation, and once it is gone it is very hard to regain." It sounded right to him. He had only his baby sister, and she was only ten now, but he knew it was far more important for the girls to act with proper decorum. No problem where Emma was concerned, and Trey's sweet wife, Carol Sue Gossman, now Carol Sue Casey, was a very proper and respectable young lady. He had loved her from afar since he was a teenager. The fact that she would marry him, a one-armed man, was a godly blessing that Trey would always hold dear.

When he had Sugar taken care of, he decided to start his search for the missing Zoe by paying the Jenkins a visit. They lived less than a mile off the main road, just outside Tampico on the way to Freetown. Mr. and Mrs. Jenkins were good, God-fearing people. There was no accounting for their sons, however. It was as though they were someone else's sons. Adam was the youngest and had two older brothers. They had been in and out of trouble their entire lives. They just seemed to have an overactive attraction to the things that caused problems for themselves as well as for others.

Trey well remembered, the oldest brother, James, who was always the first one to pick a fight with anyone he could find. Trey basically stayed out of his way. Not because he didn't want to fight James, but because it made no sense. Why fight over nothing – just to be fighting?

Mr. Jenkins came out of the house and waved to Trey, "What brings you out our way, Trey? Did my wife order something from your dad's store that I don't know about?" Mr. Jenkins was a pleasant person, and made light conversation in a friendly way.

"No, sir, Mr. Jenkins, I'm actually looking for my sister Zoe."

"Why would she be out here?"

"I don't know that she is. It's just that she didn't come home after school and Margie . . . uhhhh my mother, was worried about her." Jacob said that he had seen Zoe with

Adam several times recently. Trey knew he was opening a *can of worms*. He didn't know how else to explain.

"My goodness, are you talking about your little sister?"

"Zoe, yes, she's not the youngest though. She's in the middle. She's just thirteen and she sure shouldn't be doing things on her own."

"I know what you mean. The youngins sure take things in their own hands these days. Come on in, Trey, let me ask the Missus if she's seen Adam."

"Well, Mr. Jenkins, I don't really have time. Just tell me. Is Adam on foot or is he on horseback?"

"He left this morning on his horse, Trey. He has chores to do too – he should have come home before now. I'm sorry, Trey, I don't know what to do to help you. When he comes in, I'll have him ride over to your place."

"No, that's okay, Mr. Jenkins, I'm sure everything will turn out all right."

Trey really hoped that would be true. He sounded convincing, but he wasn't convinced himself. As he rode back down the lane to the road he saw Adam coming. Zoe wasn't with him, but then he really didn't expect that. Trey urged Dauntless to a trot and encountered Adam half way down the lane.

Trey was rather abrupt as he reined Dauntless in, "Adam, I'm looking for Zoe. Have you seen her?"

"Well, uhhhh, I did see her for a while after school. I guess she's at home."

Adam knew exactly where she was, and he knew where she had been. He was anxious to get on around Trey and out of his way.

"Was she with you, Adam?" Trey backed Dauntless around to block Adam's way.

"I gave her a ride home. If that's what you mean?"

"Well, you must have gone the long way home, because she was almost two hours late. In fact her mother went looking for her and had a terrible accident in her buggy. She has broken bones and God knows what else. So, there's lots of trouble afoot, Adam, and I think you are in the big middle of it. You better get your story straight! With that bit of *warning* advice, Trey was off, giving Dauntless a strong, "let's go nudge in the flanks!"

Trey raced back into town and went directly to the house. Zoe was there and he had a quick word with Jacob and Emma, instructing them to keep an eye on her. "In fact, don't let her out of your sight," was his parting shot. Emma, Clayton and Abby were really upset over their mother. Trey assured them that she was in good hands and would be just fine. *Oh, God, let that be true.*

As he rode up to Doctor Cumming's office, he saw his father coming out the front door. He vaulted down from the saddle and rushed up to his dad. "How is she? How is Margie?"

"She's doing as well as could be expected. Doc is getting ready to set the bones in her arm and leg. He says they are clean breaks, and with a little luck and a lot of prayer and no infections, she should be good as new. Did you find Zoe?"

"Yes, she's home. I rode out to the Jenkins and ran into Adam as I left. I pretty much pinned him down."

"What do you mean, Trey?"

"Well, he admitted that they had been together," Trey was blurting out all of his actions and thoughts. "He said he gave her a ride home after school. I told him it must have been the long way. Then I hope I scared him some over Margie's accident and all the trouble they've caused. I told him he had better get his story straight. I told Jacob and Emma to keep an eye on Zoe and not to let her out of their sight. Clay and Abby are really upset. Emma's holding steady. Of course Barton is just being himself."

"Thanks, Trey, good job. I'll stay with Margie then. Could you go back to the house? And, maybe . . . uhhhh maybe Carol Sue could go with you and help with the children. Tammy is a wonder, but I'm sure they are worried about their mother. I would really appreciate it."

"Sure, Dad, that's no problem. Just let us know how Margie is doing as soon as you can, I'll go by and tell Pastor Robertson. And, Dad, we'll be praying."

Trey had drawn close to God as a result of his war experiences. In fact, he knew it was by the grace of God that he had even survived. He was a solid and good young man.

~ *4* ~

"The godly walk with integrity;
blessed are their children who follow them."
Proverbs 20:7

M argie and Jason had long walked in integrity. They were honest and faithful people. Their spiritual lives were always attended to as their daily lives were filled with things of God. Margie now lay wounded as a result of her love and concern over one of her children who did not follow her. How does one account for that? How and why did Zoe decide to follow another path? Or was it decided for her?

Strange questions that deserve some thought. God speaks of the sins of the generations:

I lavish unfailing love to a thousand generations.I forgive iniquity, rebellion, and sin. But I do not excuse the guilty. I lay the sins of the parents upon their children and grandchildren; the entire family is affected—even children in the third and fourth gen-erations.

That quote comes from Exodus 34:7 and while it is during the time that God is leading Moses - as he leads God's people through the wilderness of sin – much of what takes place is a constant shaping and testing of a people whom God is seeking.

While in the Word of God a generation could be from 40 to 100 years, still when did the rebellious attitude get laid at Zoe's feet? Rebellion was her middle name and she had always been that way. Margie and Jason had spent many hours in conversation on how best to deal with Zoe. They worried about Joshua as well. He had never accepted Jesus as his Lord and Savior, but his choosing to study philosophy and religion gave them a great deal of hope. Pastor Robertson had been so very faithful throughout Josh's growing up years and that measure of kindness he had shown Josh was paying off.

~ ~ ~

Trey had gone by and checked on the Casey household. Everyone was holding steady. He quickly hitched a team to his dad's carriage and went to retrieve Carol Sue. She was beginning to worry about him. He had promised to be home several hours earlier. She hadn't heard about Margie's accident or Zoe's little excursion. She and Trey got some things together as Trey brought her up to date on all that had happened. They hurried back to his dad's place. They expected to stay the night at least.

~ ~ ~

Doctor Cummings had successfully set the broken bones in Margie's arm and leg and she was resting comfortably with some laudanum following the procedures. Renee was right at her side. Jason had gone back and forth from the doctor's office to the store to oversee the cleaning up of Margie's little buggy. People were still milling about talking about what happened. Jason had gotten word that the big wagon, their load and team, were all okay. Actually, the driver and his partner had done a remarkable job of curtailing the damage. It could have been a lot worse.

Renee was planning to spend the night at the doctor's offices. Doctor Cummings wanted to keep Margie close for at least twenty-four hours. Internal injury is always a concern. Moving her any distance so soon was not a good thing to do. Right now she needed to stay put.

"Renee . . . uhhhh Renee, is that you? Are you here with me? Where am I?" Margie was peeking through the haze that the pain, chloroform and laudanum had produced. She was pretty banged up. She had a big knot on her head and a gash right under it. Doc had put a couple of stitches in the gash.

"Yes ma'am, it is me. I am right here holding your hand. You had a pretty bad go of it. Don't worry, everything is fine. You're going to be alright."

"Zoe . . . Zoe where is Zoe?"

"She's fine, Honey. You just rest. Zoe is home safe and found. Everything is okay. Everybody's just thanking God for you . . . just rest now. You rest."

~ ~ ~

Meanwhile, the Casey household was in various stages of confusion. Trey and Carol Sue were dealing with the older ones and Tammy, dear, faithful Tammy was taking excellent care of Barton. He realized it was bedtime and it was the first night he had been separated from his mommy. Emma was trying to help Tammy by keeping Barton occupied as Tammy readied him for bed.

"But, Sissie," Barton with a very disappointed face, puckered up nearly ready to cry, "where is my mommy? She should be at home with me and daddy."

"Well, Mister Barton, you just never mind," Emma patting him and hugging him at the same time. "You just need to go *nighty-night*, and when you wake up in the morning I'll bet mommy and daddy will both be here. They may even bring you a bigggg surprise." Emma had her fingers crossed, hoping she wasn't telling too big a fib. Emma had been a second mother to Barton from the time he made his appearance on this earth. She had been so concerned for her mother. She hadn't experienced childbirth up close and personal. After all she was a young lady of almost fourteen when Barton was born. That was old enough to know something and not old enough to *know*.

Trey had challenged Jacob and Clay to a horseshoe pitching contest right after supper. Jacob always enjoyed his big brother. Carol Sue was keeping an eye on Zoe and working hard to keep Abby's spirit up. Abby was the worrier. Margie had become her mother at just five months of age, and while Abby tried to be very grownup about everything, still she worried. She knew about the accident. She knew that Margie had gone after Zoe and she didn't understand what the big rush was or why it was so urgent. She just knew that everybody was on pins and needles because *Her Dear Mother* was hurt.

~ ~ ~

It was ten pm and there were six children in bed if you could call the four older ones children. Actually, they were in various states of rest and unrest. Jacob knew what was going on, both in regard to Zoe and of course he was greatly concerned for Margie and his dad. He remembered, although he was only eight, the pain that he knew his father suffered at the loss of his mother. Jacob lived with both feet on the ground and he knew what people felt. In fact, he felt it right with them.

25

Emma and Abby had decided to sleep together. Really, Abby had decided it. Emma was her big sister and Emma was being very, very big considering that her mother was hurt so badly. She knew it was serious. She had heard Trey and Carol Sue talking out on the front porch right before bedtime. A broken arm and a broken leg and hoping, watching, praying that there were no internal injuries. *What did that mean - internal injuries?*

Clayton always did for himself whatever he, himself, wanted or needed. No one really knew what Clayton was thinking. He just seemed to find *a place* and quietly settle himself *there*. Margie wondered if he cared about anyone or anything but himself. She worried a lot about Clayton and Zoe. How much influence Bill's drinking and his defeatist attitude had on the way the twins seemed to deal with – or not deal with - life. It was as though a spirit had entered in that brought a mindset of "me first, or else." It was as though life had dealt them a really bad hand and it was everyone else's fault.

Just as Carol Sue was preparing to leave the kitchen, Zoe appeared in the doorway.

"Oh, Zoe, I thought you had gone to bed."

"I had. But, I just wanted to talk to you, Carol Sue. I need some advice."

"Really? Okay, sit down here at the table with me. We can talk."

"I need to know . . . what did I do that was so awful. Why was Mother and everybody, for that matter, so upset? I just went riding with Adam. I've done that before."

"Well, Honey, we young ladies don't just *go riding* with a young man especially without permission from a grownup. You didn't come home after school when you were supposed to and no one knew where you were."

Before Zoe could say a word, Trey appeared in the door of the kitchen. "Oh, excuse me, am I interrupting something?"

"Come on in, Trey, sit down with us. Zoe and I are talking about what happened this afternoon." Carol Sue was really relieved that Trey had happened in, or had he?

Zoe shifted in her chair. It almost appeared that she was getting up from the table, but Carol Sue reached out and put her hand over Zoe's. "Zoe, don't be upset because Trey is here. You've known him a lot longer than you've known me. He's your brother."

"Well, yes, but he's a man and . . . uhhhh . . . I think he's mad at me."

"No, Zoe," Trey quickly responded, "I'm not mad at you. I'm just worried about you. Worried that you are making some bad choices, I don't think you're thinking."

Carol Sue chimed in, "Zoe, Trey and I have been your age. We have struggled through those years of being old enough to do some things and not old enough for others. It's hard to grow up. Parents are always looking and listening to see what we're doing and where we are going. And, today, you made a bad choice, like Trey said, and you really upset everything."

With that long speech, Carol Sue, glanced at Trey as if to ask *what next? What do we say next? How much do we say?*

Zoe began to cry and Carol Sue handed her a hanky. "Zoe, I know you feel bad. We're all worried about your mother and things are really in a mess tonight. It'll be better tomorrow. We can talk more then. Trey and I will be here for as long as you need us. We can help you and you can help all of us."

"Sure, Zoe," Trey taking Carol Sue's lead softened his voice and approach. "Everything is looking better. We're all safe. Your mother is going to be all right. She was just careless because she was so worried about you, and she was a little quick on the trigger in her exit from the store. She was pretty upset and probably mad, too. That makes people do things they wouldn't ordinarily do."

"Let's just go to bed," Carol Sue halfway interrupting as Trey had started down the *blaming path* again. "If you're okay with it, Zoe, I'm going to say a prayer for all of us before we turn in."

Zoe nodded her head "yes" and Carol Sue prayed.

Our Father in Heaven, we thank you for Zoe's safe return to us. We thank you for Margie's healing. Watch over her and all of us through the night. Help us to rest and let tomorrow be a bright, new day of starting over. In Jesus Name I pray. Amen

With the "amen," Zoe loudly blew her nose and gave a big sigh. "Thanks, you two. I feel better. I'm still confused, but better. Good night."

Zoe got up and left and Trey gave Carol Sue the biggest smile you could imagine. He was a lucky man and he knew it.

~ 5 ~

*"Who is he that condemns? Christ Jesus, who
died – more than that who was raised to life
is at the right hand of God and is also
interceding for us."*
Romans 8:34

Margie had a fairly good night, considering. Renee had
kept a watchful eye on her, resting as she could. Doc
came into the office extra early to check on his patient and
his nurse.

"Well, how are you ladies this morning? Did I do a good
job or not?"

Margie opened her eyes and tried to smile. She knew
she was alive because every bone in her body ached. Renee
brought the coffee pot from the stove and poured Doc a cup
of coffee. Margie was allowed a few sips of water. Everything had gone well through the night.

"I think I'm hungry," Margie weakly quipped. "What's
for breakfast?"

"Oh, great horny toads," Doc guffawed. "I always feel
relieved when my patients start complaining about being
hungry. Broth, my girl, broth, that's what you can have for
breakfast and only a few teaspoons full."

Renee had suspected as much and had already sent Jason to the hotel to see what he could conjure up in the way of broth. Jason had slipped in the back door of Doc's offices around five am. He couldn't stand it any longer. Margie was resting and he just sat and watched her breathe for over an hour. When the sun began to rise, he stirred and stretched his long legs and he and Renee conferred to send him on his mission of finding broth.

Doc proceeded to check Margie's injuries as he tenderly palpitated her abdomen and measured, with his experienced eye, the swelling of her limbs. All seemed to be doing well. She had been healthy and active before the accident, and she would be again.

There was a slight knock at the inner door and who should appear but Jacob and Emma. They were up at daylight and had made a grown-up decision to come on by. They had run into each other in the upstairs hall on the way to the morning necessities and realized that Jason had already left the house. They didn't even have to speak of their plans. They just got ready and came. Jacob was so chivalrous, on such short notice, that he even saddled a horse for Emma. Riding double at their ages was a little too much for the two teens.

"Come in, come in," Renee invited, "your mother is awake and complaining about being hungry."

Before they could move to Margie's side, Jason appeared with the broth. He also brought some weak tea and toast. Mrs. Gruber, the hotel cook, made that decision. But, Doc would agree to liquids only for Margie for a day or so. He was just doing his job – making sure first that Margie's insides were going to work well.

"Mother," Emma dropped down beside Margie's bed, "how are you? I was so worried."

"I'm fine, Honey," Margie spoke in slightly quiet tones. "You can't keep a tough ol' bird like me down," faintly smiling as she spoke, heavy on the "ol," as if thirty-three was old. She just felt like she was eighty.

Ignoring her mother's comment, Emma *gushed* on, "Oh, I'm so relieved! Jacob and I couldn't wait – we just had to see you as soon as we could. Everything and everyone is fine at home. Trey and Carol Sue spent the night. It really helped."

Jacob moved closer and smiled down at Margie loving her and soaking into his very troubled soul a hint of some measure of wellness. He had prayed and hoped and hoped and prayed most of the night. Jacob was the "man" of the boys. He always stepped into the gap that others left.

"Well, this family reunion needs to be suspended for a while. I need to *broth* my patient and let her rest. Doctor's orders right now, not too much of anything else for a while." Renee, doing her nurse thing, began to shoo them out.

Emma bowed her head and tried not to let a tear slide down her face. She hated leaving her mother, but she knew that was best. Jacob just cleared his "manly" throat and shuffled on out – casting a smile toward Margie just in case she could see him. Jason stayed on and Renee knew that would be his choice. Jason loved Margie dearly. They were a wonderful family. They all worked so hard at appreciating God's rich blessings and spreading them throughout their growing family and the community of friends and neighbors.

~ *6* ~

**"The eternal God is your refuge, and his
everlasting arms are under you."**
Deuteronomy 33:27

George, the eternal reporter, was staying occupied
working on what the rest of the world, particularly the
nation, was doing. In the past two years, the 14th Amendment
to the Constitution granted citizenship to the Black folks and
guaranteed "equal protection of the laws" to all American
citizens. Politics was a mess in the country, the attempt to
impeach Present Johnson failed by only one vote. The next
presidential election saw Ulysses S. Grant inaugurated as the
18th president. In 1870 the ninth census of the U. S. population totaled almost 40 million. Five million were Blacks and
two plus million were immigrants who have arrived in the
previous decade.

The 15th Amendment to the Constitution was favored to
pass that would grant suffrage to Black men. Times were
changing rapidly, but the recovering nation was struggling.
Congress was sponsoring a bill to stop southern white resis-
tance to the power that Blacks had gained during Reconstruction. The "Enforcement Act," or "Ku Klux Klan Act

of 1870" had become very controversial even in the border states.

George was in constant motion, reading, writing, traveling as he could to gather news and keep his finger on the pulse of the community and the nation. He had become a managing partner in the Tampico Tribune over the past nine years. He and Renee had settled into the community and become vital citizens of the burgeoning southern Indiana city. Manufacturing and commerce had recovered in the area and the economy was growing.

~ ~ ~

Martin and Rose were faithful to stay in touch. Rose and Renee exchanged letters several times a month. Martin was doing well in his appointment at West Point as the Commanding General's Surgeon. Barton "Patrick" Smallwood had turned five in January of 1870, but the best part was two little sisters who had been born in the past three years.

Marilyn Rose was three and Sally Renee was two. Needless to say, Martin and Rose were very busy with their growing family. They had planned to travel west to Indiana after Marilyn Rose was old enough, but surprise! Sally was on the way. Life was good and all was well. The unrest in the far west was their biggest concern.

While the "War Between the States" was being fought between 1860 and 1865 the Indian tribes of the West were rising up in greater numbers than ever before. They claimed that emigrants moving west were slaughtering bison and other game. Unfortunately, it was true. "Bad Faith" was the title given the breaking of many treaties.

George was particularly interested in the reports of the Plains Indians acquiring great amounts of firearms and horses from the wagon trains. The stage lines were constantly in danger and the mail was interrupted to the extent that at one point the stagecoach station at Latham, Colorado, had accumulated about three tons of sacked mail.

If Renee had not held a tight rein on George and his passion to collect the news, he would have been in the big middle of it. The Union Army was severely taxed trying to keep up with the need for Army posts all along the Overland Trail. Even that was not able to keep the stagecoaches running. George was just grateful that Martin's assignment had overridden his need to be deployed to the West and its Indian Wars.

Another great story of interest was the state of Wyoming giving women the right to vote in 1869. That was the first enacted legislation allowing women's suffrage and, it was a hard fought battle. It would not stop there. Politics, citizens rights, Indian uprisings, reconstruction of the South, just recovery in general from the war to end all wars, kept everyone and everything hard-pressed to keep up.

~ ~ ~

Speaking of keeping up, Jason was having a grand time corralling all of the children, especially keeping a wary eye on Zoe. Margie had been moved to the house after three days at the Doctor's office. She was comfortable and well cared for, however, not happy with her confinement. Tammy was always the angel on duty, and Trey and Carol Sue were a godsend.

Carol Sue had become a wise counsel to Zoe, and Zoe seemed to thrive on Carol Sue's grace and wisdom. Margie was somewhat aware of the situation, but as long as Zoe was accounted for she could at least rest about that situation. That is Zoe's whereabouts for now. Margie mostly tried to "mother" Baby Barton and get him settled back into a schedule that was manageable. He had the worst time of all with his mother missing for three days.

~ 7 ~

"You will keep in perfect peace all who trust in you, all whose thoughts are fixed on you!"
Isaiah 26:3

Joshua had come home for the summer and was working in the store. Business was booming. The notable change in Joshua though was not his growing into a *bonafide* store-keeper. The notable change in Joshua was that he had grown into a believer in the Lord Jesus Christ. It was rather subtle. He didn't talk about it. The mystery was the tremendous change in his spiritual beliefs. Growing up, especially after his mother's death when Abby was born, he absolutely resented any mention of God or God's part in creation and life. Now, he moved about with a grace and a faith that was almost enviable.

Margie mentioned it to Jason about a week after Joshua had come home for the summer. "Yes, you're right, Margie, there seems to be a big change in our son, Joshua, and his attitude toward God. Amazing! Don't get me wrong, I am so very grateful. It seems our prayers have been answered where Joshua is concerned. Now, if we could get some sense working in Zoe's brain and spirit. Then if we could see

Clayton's heart changed to a life with resolve toward *hope with a future* . . . well, we would be home free."

"Well, Dearest Husband, with nine children to rear, I would say that we have been especially blessed in all of them. I will be eternally grateful for all that God is doing in our family."

With that little speech Margie was just about asleep. She had been up hobbling about on one crutch with her good arm. Jason couldn't keep her down. No one could ever keep Margie down. She inherited that good quality from the long line of strong women in her family. Of course her greatest time of sorrow and pain had been the deaths of four loved ones in her brief life. There was the loss of her little brother, Barton, followed by Uncle Maurey's tragic death and Bill's horrible accident that took his life, not to mention losing her dear mother much too soon. However, in her growing up time, she had watched her mother and her father live through Barton and Maurey's death with a great and strong faith in God and the future that he had planned for them. What was that verse that her mother always, quoted something about *God said, I know the plans I have for you . . . Plans to give you hope and a future.*

"Good night, Dear, God bless. I love you." With that sleepy little speech Margie was sound asleep. Jason gave her a sweet kiss on the forehead and silently thanked God for his wonderful wife. Especially giving thanks that she had survived that horrible accident.

Jason went back downstairs to check the doors and the lamps and see where all and who all had finally made it to bed. Baby Barton had been sound asleep for some time. Usually Abby and Emma were at least busy in their room if they hadn't finally given up and gone to sleep. They were sharing a room for the summer with Joshua home. Needless to say, that caused a lot of female chatter. Jacob and Clay were billeted together and Zoe had decided that she would rather be a sleeping partner in the baby's room than share with the other girls.

As Jason turned the corner from the hall, coming out of the front part of the house, he ran into Joshua who had treated himself to a cold glass of milk and some freshly baked cookies. "Oh, excuse me, Dad, I didn't see you coming. Did I spill milk on you?"

" No son, you didn't. Wanta try again? " laughing Jason stepped back.

"Actually, I'm just glad it wasn't coffee. That could have been worse." Joshua could joke too. He smiled a big smile at his dad and acted as though he would go on up the stairs.

"Uhhhh, Joshua, why don't you come back in the kitchen and have a chat with me? I could go for some milk and cookies too."

"Sure, Dad, what do you want to chat about?"

That was it. That was an *opportunity* to talk to Joshua about his change of heart. Why, where and how had this transformation come about? Jason was thinking hard to get a line on how to ask Joshua about the big change without causing him to be uncomfortable or defensive.

"I just wanted to catch up with you, Son. With all the activity around this family there is never an opportunity to just sit down and visit one-on-one."

"Great! I'm into talking these days. I don't know if you and *Mother* noticed that I'm different. I guess you could say grown up."

"Well, as a matter of fact," as Jason poured himself a glass of milk with his back to Joshua and his face plastered with a smile that could almost be heard, "we have noticed that you indeed are becoming a man. And, I might add a very pleasant and amiable one."

"Thanks, Dad. That's good news. I wasn't sure that anyone would recognize me. You see my change is from the inside out. I've made Jesus Christ my personal savior and my life has changed."

"Hummmm," Jason was feeling joy and surprise and didn't have any words. Finding his voice, "Oh, my, Joshua, that's wonderful." *Mercy! Lord! Wonderful doesn't seem to be a strong enough word for celebration.*

"I know! I know! I wanted to tell you as soon as I got home but I didn't know how to start. I've been praying that the Lord would give me the *opportunity.*"

There's that word that Jason had prayed for. *Opportunity.*

"Well, Son, there is nothing in the world that could make me happier as your father AND your brother in Christ. Praise God, Joshua! Praise God!"

Joshua got up from the table and hugged his dad with the love of God pouring through his embrace. They sat down and finished their "midnight treat," and then said a quick "good night," and the two brothers in Christ departed for a peaceful and joyous rest.

Jason couldn't go to sleep thinking about Joshua. *Joshua fit the battle of Jericho, Jericho, Jericho – Joshua fit the battle of Jericho, and the walls came tumblin' down.*

The hardest part was waiting until morning to tell Margie. He could hardly lie down and lie still for his heart was just jumping with joy. Joshua had found the Lord and his life would now be so different. Peace, joy, wisdom, patience – gifts and fruits of the Spirit of the Living God. AMEN!

~ 8 ~

*"The Lord said, 'Make thankfulness your
sacrifice to God, and keep the vows you made to
the Most High. Then call on me when you are in
trouble, and I will rescue you, and you will
give me glory.'"*
Psalm 50:14-15

Margie was propped up in the kitchen, peeling apples for a couple of apple pies. One pie was never enough for that bunch. Where did she find her strength? It was Jason's wonderful love and devotion, not to mention the much needed physical assistance that kept Margie going as she healed. Jason carefully helped her negotiate the stairs before he left for work. Actually, he gently carried her down the stairs.

She was still thinking about their waking conversation. It was more like a celebrative time of praise and worship. Jason could hardly wait for Margie to stir and he even gave her some time as he helped her sit up and take account of her cramped and barely rested body. With one leg propped up on pillows and her arm cocooned as well she was lucky that she slept at all. She just really couldn't get good rest. Doctor Cumming's orders were six weeks of the splints and the casts. She was half way. She was always bone-tired when she went to bed – but after several hours it was a chore to even stay in bed.

"Jason, Honey, tell me again. What did Joshua say?"

"Well, he just came right out and said that he had given his life to Jesus Christ as his Lord and Savior. Then we embraced and his joy was so authentic. He is a different person, Margie. He has found the secret to the happy life in Christ Jesus."

Margie and Jason had a prayer together giving thanks to God for Joshua's decision. What is it about seeing your loved ones, especially your children, find that *peace that passes understanding ?* Experiencing it secondhand for someone else is almost as good as your own elation. Can you imagine God's elation?

~ ~ ~

Zoe, dear Zoe . . . she had made some unbelievable headway talking with and listening to Carol Sue. Zoe had lived in Emma's shadow from the time she was born. Emma was the first born, only by one year, but it made a big difference, and Emma was always confident and busy about life. Zoe tried to follow in her footsteps, but it just wasn't working. Carol Sue had been so amazing to *listen, listen and love, love*. It was a natural thing for Carol Sue. It truly was *Amazing Grace*. God was working so . . .so . . . well just like God. The miracle was that the young people were in tune and willing.

As Carol Sue patiently found time and ways to encourage Zoe, the Holy Spirit was always there with the promises of God's Word - interceding for us:

In the same way, the Spirit helps us in our weakness. We do not know what we ought to pray for, but the Spirit himself intercedes for us with groans that words cannot express. And he who searches our hearts knows the mind of the Spirit, because the Spirit intercedes for the saints in accordance with God's will. (Romans 8:26-27)

Things began to change for Zoe. Summer was a wonderful time of laughter and fun. Joshua, Jacob, Emma and Zoe were nearly inseparable. Theirs was a teenage bonanza. Picnics, games and of course church was in the center of all their activities. It seemed as though the whole family had taken Zoe's *near miss* to heart. The young people, in particular, seemed to rally 'round Zoe to insure her confidence and safety.

The Church Baseball League of Tampico was a big deal. Both Joshua and Jacob played on their church's team. Emma, Zoe, Abby and Clay were their biggest fans, and often the whole family made it to the games. Well, except Mother Margie. She and the Barton stayed behind. It was the best thing for all – that is Margie's health and everyone else's peace.

The young people gathered as often as they could for refreshments at someone's home. The Caseys were the biggest supporters of that delightful time. Conversations and flirtations ran rampant with games and food a close second. Jeremy and his friends often joined in at least it gave those moving toward marriage a place to socialize.

~ 9 ~

*"Come, my children, listen to me; I will teach you
the fear of the LORD. Whoever of you
loves life and desires to see many good
days, keep your tongue from evil and
your lips from speaking lies."*
Psalm 34:11-13

Jeremy had joined his father and Trey with management of the store and its recent expansion. They were doing business all over the county and had even established themselves as distributors of several lines of small farm implements. George's help with Casey's Emporium had slowed down considerably especially with his passion for the newspaper business. Jason was glad to have his two oldest sons in the business and it gave him time to enjoy Margie and the younger children, not to mention his continuing interest in the breeding of the American Saddle Horse. The first County Fair since the end of the civil War would be held the summer of 1871. Jason was grooming a mare and a stallion for competition in the racing events.

While horses and fairs had always been important in Jeremy's life, they were playing second fiddle for Jeremy those days. Jeremy had discovered someone perfectly wonderful.

Alvina Ashton was Jeremy's discovery. She had grown up in Seymour where her father was the Methodist Episcopal Church pastor. She was named for him, Reverend Alvin Lloyd Ashton. She was an only child of her dear parents and had kept house for her father since the death of her mother some five years earlier. She and Jeremy were in their early twenties. So, Alvina, "Alvey," as she had always been fondly called, happily served as her father's housekeeper and cook since her early teens. She was one of the dearest young ladies around. Jeremy met her when he accompanied Trey on a delivery to Seymour several months ago. The church had purchased quite a bit of lumber and hardware to make some much needed repair that the war had caused.

A rather insignificant firefight had ensued between Union and Confederate soldiers. The Army of the South was always hard pressed for food and shelter. It seems that a roaming and detached patrol of Confederates had taken shelter in the church, and when they were discovered the battle was on. However, the little battle was very significant to the church. There were holes in the walls and missing windows, not to mention the wrecked front door. The parishioners had done their best to make some satisfactory repairs, but it needed to be properly restored.

Rev. Ashton had approached Jason's store to furnish the needed materials to make the repairs. Jason Casey was known far and wide to be a fair and generous man to deal with. He had given the church his profit in the purchase and provided the transportation to deliver the materials.

Alvey just happened to be at the church. She and her father were preparing for the Sunday services on the Saturday of the delivery. As divine providence would have it, there appeared the man God had chosen for her. Alvey saw Jeremy before he saw her. He and Trey were in the back, behind the church, unloading the wagon. Her father had walked outside to oversee the unloading and she had followed him. There he was. Who could have missed that six foot, three inch frame and the gorgeous, curly red hair? She was embarrassed at her own reaction. She felt her face flush as her heart skipped a beat. She hoped no one else noticed it. Alvey quickly walked back into the church and busied herself with the dusting in the sanctuary.

She had just finished when her father came through from the back door looking for her. "Alvina, where are you? I thought you were out back with me."

"I'm right here, Father. I needed to get the sanctuary finished."

"Well, that can wait. I've invited the Casey boys over to the parsonage. I thought they should take a minute and have some tea and some of that delicious cake you made for us yesterday."

"Oh, Father, the house is not fit for company. I still have dishes from breakfast and furniture pulled out from my cleaning . . . I really wish you hadn't invited them in."

"Nonsense, Alvina, come on. They need to get on back to Tampico. I just wanted to say thank you."

With that argument over, Alvey and her dad hurried on across the lawn to meet the Caseys as they came around the corner of the church. Jeremy saw Alvina at this juncture. For sure he SAW her. How could anyone miss her? She was a tall girl, but very poised and very pretty. Alvina had natural blonde hair and a radiant glow. Her complexion was an indication of her heart and soul, clear and beautiful. Her eyes were grey-blue, and she had dimples that you couldn't miss. She smiled as her father introduced Trey and Jeremy to her. Trey couldn't help but notice that Jeremy was sure paying attention in a new and wonderful way.

Reverend Ashton led the boys through the back door into the kitchen and invited them to take a seat at the kitchen table. After all they were in their work clothes and not really making a formal call.

"I can't thank you enough. Please convey to your father our deep appreciation for his generosity. We have been scrimping and saving for several years to make these repairs. After all, the Lord's House deserves to be in cared for. Wouldn't you agree?"

"Yes sir," Trey chirped. "Absolutely, right."

Both he and Jeremy were somewhat uncomfortable. They really needed to get back to Tampico. It seemed these days they were busy from morning to night with either stocking or deliveries. Mostly the cause of their unrest was the beautiful young woman flitting about preparing their small repast. Trey wasn't really uncomfortable. He was just aching to tease Jeremy. It was obvious that Jeremy was smitten.

Tea and cake were served, and Alvey tried to excuse herself. She mumbled something about Saturday and Sunday and how much she still had to do. Her father looked up, thinking, *what is the matter with that girl? She isn't usually so jittery.* It didn't occur to him that *love was in the air.* Or at least sparks were flying.

Trey gave Jeremy a slight kick under the table as if to say, *"Don't just sit there, say something."*

Jeremy flinched and turned to look at Trey who winked at him. Trey gave a sideward nod toward Alvey's departing figure and Jeremy jerked around in her direction and in a halfway squeaky voice blurted out, "Thank you, Miss Ashton for the *cea and take*, I mean tea and cake it was . . . I mean it is delicious."

Trey almost spit his bite of cake straight into the air. He managed to swallow and quickly took a sip of tea. He had never seen his little brother so bum fuddled.

They finished their little mid-morning treat and made a quick exit. Alvey was standing behind the curtain in her bedroom, peeking out at as she watched them depart. *What had happened? Was he real? I need to pinch myself and see if I'm still alive.*

As the wagon turned the corner – Trey reached over and slapped Jeremy on the back. He didn't need two arms to give Jeremy the manly thumping. "Well, ol' boy, whadda you think? Seymour has some fine scenery – wouldn't you say. I mean the right age, good looking, single and dimples from heaven. Obviously, she can cook and keep house – you'd better get right busy, Little Brother."

Jeremy slapped the reins and grunted. He really didn't know what to say.

~ *10* ~

*"He has given me a new song to sing, a hymn of
praise to our God. Many will see what he
has done and be amazed. They will put their
trust in the Lord."*
Psalm 40:3

Joe Ramsey entered the front door of Casey's Emporium
looking for George. The clerk up front told him that
George wasn't there. In fact, he wasn't even in town. "Well,"
Joe whined, "what do you think I *oughta* do with this here
telegram? It just *come* for George Smallwood and I think it's
purty important. It came from West Point." Joe wasn't the
regular messenger to carry telegrams. He didn't like it when
Tom Barkman was not available and he had to get up off the
town bench and try to find the recipient of whatever missal
he was trying to deliver. Joe really preferred to just sit on the
bench outside the telegraph office and talk with the other *ner
do wells* that called the bench home.

"Why don't you go upstairs to the office and ask Mr.
Casey?" the clerk answered Joe.

"Yeah, right, that's a good *idie*. I'll *jest* do that."

With that affirmative response, Joe climbed the stairs and knocked on the office door at the end of the hall. "Come in," Jason called out. "Oh, Joe, what can I do for you?"

"Well, Mr. Casey, this here telegram *come* for George Smallwood. I was *hopin'* he was here."

"No, Joe, he's on a buying trip for me. You probably should take it to Mrs. Smallwood, you know, Renee. She's at Doctor Cumming's office."

"Oh, all right," Joe answered as he turned in a dejected little circle, muttering to himself as he descended the stairs. *I swear, it's gettin' harder and harder to deeeeliver a tellllee-gram to folks. They ain't never whar they're supposed to be.* Renee was in the examination room with Dr. Cummings when Joe got to the doc's office. He waited for her to come out to call the next patient – then he practically attacked her as he thrust the telegram into her hand. "Here! This is *fer* your husband. I been *chasin'* around all over town *tryin'* to find him. You give it to him." With a disgusted attitude, Joe turned and bolted out of the office. *Never mind a tip – I'm jest glad to git shut of it!* Joe again muttering to himself.

Renee unfolded the message and saw that it was from West Point. *Oh, Lord, I hope it's not bad news . . . Rose and the babies and Martin . . .* it wasn't. She scanned it quickly and was very relieved to find that it was merely an invitation from Martin for George to join him on an excursion into the Indian Territory . . . *Relieved! What in the world is Martin talking about?. Why would George want to do that?* Immediately she wished she hadn't read it. *Now,* she was worried. Only five minutes before she had been perfectly happy. Telegrams hardly ever make things better.

George was due back the next day around noon. It would just have to wait until then. It wasn't addressed to her anyway. *Indian Territory? These Smallwood men . . . they were beyond belief.* George was always on the cutting edge of things. As a journalist, his first love was writing. He was constantly looking for a good story. Unlike Rally Butler, Renee's first husband, George was industrious, interesting and always willing to be of service for anyone who needed help. She decided it was a pretty good trade-off though. Sense and sensibility in a man vs. laziness and self-indulgence, however, George was never in one place very long. She missed him!

George got home on time the next day and the telegram actually read:

Dad. Trip to spend three months in West.
Permission for you to come as correspondent. Can
you go?
Leaving two weeks. Martin

Renee watched as George read the missal. He gave a large sigh as he looked up and realized that Renee was watching him. "Well, what do you know? Martin is branching out. I wonder why he's been appointed to go out there?"

"Probably it has something to do with medicine. I mean, well, why else would they ask a doctor to do that?" Renee offered.

"Sure, that has to be it. I know that the reports have been coming in for months and months about the activity of the Indian Nations. In fact, I just read in a paper from the east coast that the "Indian Appropriations Act" has ended the policy of recognizing the Indian tribes as sovereign nations."

"My goodness, George, what does all that mean?" Renee asked

"Well, Honey, it means that the Indians have legally become wards of America. That is they have been forced to come under the law and the government. Indian policy will be made through the legislature and executive order. Basically, they don't have much input into their own lives."

"That doesn't seem fair, George. How can the government do that?" Renee was asking innocently. Really she just wasn't aware of all the violence and hardships that were being lodged upon both the settlers and the Indians. It had been an ongoing conflict, fraught with considerable loss of life and property on both sides.

George didn't want to say too much about the violence. Of course, he was chomping at the bit to go with Martin. How often does a writer/reporter/story teller/father/grandfather get a chance like that?

Renee broke the lull with a big sigh as she wheeled around and said, "Well, don't need to think about all that tonight. You just got home and I've got to fix supper."

"Right!" George agreed. It was easier to just "ease" out of the conversation for now and back off so he could form a plan of attack. Gaining Renee's permission and blessing for a three month expedition into Indian Territory was going to be the biggest challenge he would probably face in the whole deal.

"Uhhhh, I've got to go by the store, Renee. I'll be back within an hour. That won't make supper late, will it, Dear?" On his best behavior, George just needed to exit and avoid anymore conversation about the trip for now.

"Okay, George, an hour will be fine." Renee knew what he was up to. His demeanor had changed and his extremely careful choice of words was telling. *She hadn't come into town on a load of logs.* In other words Renee had been around men and their manipulations for most of her life. She mused *George, George, do you think I don't know you are dying to go with Martin? You're handling me with "kid gloves." That's good! I like being convinced.*

~ *11* ~

"The love of the LORD remains forever with those who fear him. His salvation extends to the children's children of those who are faithful to his covenant, of those who obey his commandments!"
Psalm 103:17-18

Zoe and Joshua had spent several opportune moments together. The summer was in full swing, and they were busy along with the whole family. It just always seemed that they ended up in the same place at the same time. Josh's college experience had given him an edge as for conversation and a more mature approach to life and its challenges. Zoe had shared with him her troublesome behavior. He explained to her that being a part of a large family often brought on loneliness that was unexpected and even painful.

As they sat on the front porch one Sunday after dinner, Zoe turned to Joshua with tears ready to slide down her cheeks, "Joshua, I haven't told anyone how horrible I feel about my mother's accident. You know she was looking for me when it happened. Every time I see her so painfully hobbling around the house I just want to burst into tears and run from the room."

"Have you told her how you feel, Zoe? That's one thing I have learned in the last two years. I've found that being honest with myself, as well as with others, has given me a new lease on life."

"What do you mean, Joshua, *a new lease on life*? I don't understand. Wasn't your life good when you were still home, here, living with all of us?"

"My life was okay, Zoe, it's just that I wasn't okay. I didn't understand or realize that there was love enough for all of us. I didn't appreciate the fact that Dad and your mother, Margie, loved us with an unconditional and abiding love. I didn't have any idea that they were one hundred per cent for us kids and everything they did was to help us."

"My goodness, is that true? I mean do they love us all the same? I've never felt that way. I've always thought that Mother loved Emma the most. After all Emma is the smartest and the prettiest."

"Really, says who, Miss Zoe? Did you take a survey? How did you come to that conclusion?"

"Oh, Josh, you're teasing me. You know what I mean. Emma never gets in trouble. She always says the right things at the right times. Everyone loves Emma."

"That's what I'm talking about, Zoe. You are stuck in your own mind. You are your own worst enemy. The reason I know that is because I was that way too."

"I don't believe that, Joshua, you have always been sure and strong."

"No, I haven't. You were younger during those years. Let's see you were three when you came to live here and I was almost eleven. You were too little to know what it was like to be part of this huge, disconnected family. I had two older brothers who were always with Dad. Jacob was cute and smart, and our new baby sister seemed to have all the attention. My mother had just died and I was just left out there . . . really all alone in the midst of a crowd."

"Oh, Joshua, I had no idea. My entire life, or at least since I can remember, I have felt like I was invisible. I guess that's why I've always been such a show-off, I mean just to prove that I'm not invisible."

"Well, we do funny things that we're not even aware of, and Zoe, there's one more thing. What I'm about to tell you has meant more to me than anything I have ever experienced. What has happened to me has changed my life completely. In the past year, I have come to know Jesus Christ as my personal savior. That's the one thing in life that makes all the difference. I know that I am never alone. I know that I am forgiven. I know that God goes before me and that God has a plan for my life, for my life, Zoe. . . for my life."

"Hey, you two is this a private party or can anyone join in?" Jacob sauntered out on to the porch and perched on the porch railing. He could see and feel that the conversation had been very serious, and he immediately regretted that he had crashed their conversation.

"Mr. Jacob," Josh half sang the greeting, "you are always welcome in my world, Brother."

Jacob grinned. He just couldn't get used to Josh's new personality. He knew or had overheard that Joshua had made a decision for Jesus, but he still couldn't become accustomed to the drastic change in Joshua's attitude and presence.

Zoe got up from the swing and curtsied as though she was making one of her dramatic exits. She had felt inclined to talk to Joshua about her younger years and habit of showing off. She was embarrassed to think about it now. But, she knew the conversation was over for at least at this sitting. She only hoped it could happen again. She really appreciated Joshua's friendship. A lot!

In her performance mode, Zoe exclaimed, "Fare thee well, my fine friends. I am off to charm the world." With that flirting flair, Zoe departed.

~ 12 ~

***"Take courage as you fulfill your duties, and may
the LORD be with those who do what is right."***
2 Chronicles 19:11

George and Renee had talked a little. It had been almost
a whole day and night since the telegram came. He
needed to get an answer to Martin about whether or not he
was going with him. He didn't know exactly why the trip.
He knew it had to be about doctoring, but whatever it was
about he truly wanted to be there. He could interview, have
discussions and document lots of important information
that needed to be recorded. Actually, there was no limit to
journalistic opportunities. When ink flows in the veins, the
writer is fully alive.

Renee was not convinced, although she was a great deal
more understanding than George was expecting. "George, I
know you're stewing about accompanying Martin on this trip
out west. I also know how much you want to go," Renee paused
and turned to George as she spoke, "Honey, I'll miss you."

"Oh, Renee!" George turned to Renee and took her
hands, "Oh, Renee, does this mean you're saying it's all
right if I go?"

"Honey, as I said, I'll miss you. You have to promise me you won't take any chances and that you'll come home in one piece **with** your scalp."

They both laughed as George planted a sweet and thankful kiss on Renee's forehead followed by a huge embrace.

Renee patted George's face as she backed away, "All right, Mr. Smallwood, I need to get supper on the table. You can probably still get a telegram off to Martin if you hurry. Just get back quickly supper will be ready."

~ ~ ~

Martin was excited when he received his dad's telegram the next day. He responded immediately, briefly giving details of the assignment and the time schedule. They were to leave by the end of the month, which was only two weeks away. Their mission was to establish some training criteria for medical personnel in the area. There weren't enough doctors to have sufficient medical coverage in the outlying Army posts. There was a lot of activity along the line of the Army defenses, mostly stationed on or near the Overland Trail. Martin's experience in the War Between the States was a valuable asset to the battlefield care that was needed in the west.

George discussed it all with Jason the next morning and Jason was in total agreement. He had Trey and Jeremy and the regular staff of folks in the store. He assured George that everything there would not suffer because he was absent.

Actually, George was more concerned about Margie's healing. He had spent a great deal of time helping her move about. They also renewed their long chats that they both had so enjoyed over the years. Most of their discussion was about the family and their needs.

"You were too little to remember," George was reminiscing about the days in Mitchell when the three children were so close, "you were the dependable one, Margie. Little-grown-up-Margie. So serious, so helpful, always knowing what needed to be done. I swear your mother said many times that you could have run the household."

Margie laughed thinking back over the years. Tears began to form in her eyes as she recalled her dear mother. Emma was a dear, dear person. Everyone loved Emma. That couldn't be said for her older sister, Stella. Stella had been burdened with all the responsibility of rearing that family when both of their parents had died. Emma was so little and being the baby was coddled. She hadn't become spoiled. She just had a very sweet nature, capable, but sweet.

"I remember one time, Dad, when I decided that I could cook. I had watched mother every day. I decided mashed potatoes would be good and I fetched the potatoes from the cellar, got a paring knife and a pot of water and set about peeling potatoes. By the time mother came home from the lady's meeting at church I had six or seven little knots left. Most of the potatoes were hooked to the peelings. Mother didn't scold me, she told me that peeling potatoes was very hard to do and she was a teenager before she could peel a potato and have some left to cook."

George was a great comfort to Margie and a wonderful grandfather to all the kids, the Caseys, the Wilsons and the Smallwoods. There were twelve of them to be exact, counting Martin's three. He figured it wouldn't be too long until he would be a great grandfather. Trey and Carol Sue had been married several years and it was time for them to start their family. Little did he or Margie know that the announcement had not yet been made, but it was forth coming. The younger Casey's were expecting and decided to make the big announcement at Sunday dinner.

~ *13* ~

"For since the creation of the world God's
invisible qualities – his eternal power and divine
nature – have been clearly seen,
being understood from what has been made,
so that men are without excuse."
Romans 1:20

George's upcoming adventure was the talk of Sunday dinner. Jacob was particularly interested in "Grandpa" George's exciting opportunity. Jacob sat by George and pelted him with questions throughout the meal. Renee and Carol Sue had been stepping up to help Tammy since Margie's accident. However, today Carol Sue was just not up to par. Renee suspected something was going on, but she kept quiet.

With George leaving a week from next Saturday, he only would be home for one more Sunday dinner. Renee tried not to think about that, and was praying constantly for his safe return before he had even left. Of course, she included Rose, the children and Martin in her prayers. One good thing that occurred from all of this excitement was the fact that Rose and the children were coming with Martin as he picked up his dad and began the trek west. In fact the four of them would be staying on in Tampico. It would be a three month visit.

Dessert had been served when Trey stood up, clinked his glass with his knife, cleared his throat and said, "Dad, Margie, are you ready to be grandparents?" A big cheer went up around the table. Trey took Carol Sue's arm and pulled her to her feet. "Here she is, mother-to-be." As Carol Sue stood up Trey gave her a big hug. Everyone was talking at once and Jason reached over to cover Margie's hand as he smiled at her and whispered, "Honey, you are going to be one of the youngest grandmothers around, but I dare say one of the dearest and prettiest."

"Oh, Jason, I'm so happy for them. They are as solid as a rock. They'll make wonderful parents."

"When, Trey, when is the baby coming?" Zoe had found her voice. She felt particularly close to Trey and Carol Sue. They had continued their "big brother/big sister" role with Zoe and Zoe had matured by leaps and bounds. All the grown-ups had been making sly comments to each other regarding Josh and Zoe anyway. They both had changed so much. Joshua shone with his commitment to a life in Christ and Zoe was glowing with a renewed and joyous commitment to life. It was all good, and there was more to come.

To answer Zoe's questions, which of course, everyone wanted to know. Trey winked at Carol Sue and said, "Well, the doctor figures sometime in March . . . I know that's a spell down the road, but to tell you the truth, I couldn't wait any longer to "crow!" Everyone laughed and thoroughly enjoyed Trey and Carol Sue's happiness.

Jeremy was next to speak. He didn't stand up to gain everyone's attention, but because Jeremy hardly ever called attention to himself, it wasn't difficult for everyone to quiet down enough to hear him tell of his plans. He blushed as he asked if he could invite some special guests next Sunday. The get-together had been planned for the afternoon as it would be George and Martin's launching party. In fact, they had gotten word that the Martin Smallwoods would be in Tampico late Saturday afternoon. They were coming by train and the whole family was celebrating each in his or her own way. So, it would really be a brief but exciting Homecoming and a Bon Voyage for George and Martin.

Margie was paying attention to help Jeremy make his little speech, "Absolutely, Jeremy, you can have special guests. Who might he or she be?"

Jeremy's blush deepened as he described Alvina and her father, Reverend Ashton.

"We met when Trey and I delivered the lumber to the church in Seymour, Reverend Ashton's church."

Trey didn't say a word. He was being particularly kind, considering that he would really like to put Jeremy on the spot and embarrass him or at least tease him about his newly discovered *heartthrob*. Becoming an expectant father had matured Trey considerably. His usual *embarrass your siblings every chance you get* had waned. He felt paternal toward Jeremy, as opposed to the raucous, tantalizing older brother that he had always been with his three younger brothers.

"I met Alvina Ashton," Jason offered. "She's a mighty nice looking young lady, Jeremy. You have good taste." With that little tidbit thrown out, the "ooh's" and the "ahh's" were being murmured all around the table. Even Clay joined in. Emma and Zoe nudged each other, as they enjoyed any conversation about romance and "love." The girls loved to talk about love.

"Are you gonna' marry her?" Abby's eight-year-old innocence braved the question. With that a spontaneous verbal outburst came from the young people. Jeremy looked like he had swallowed a camel and everyone had a good chuckle before Jeremy could again clear his throat and speak. Margie came to his rescue again, "Stop it, all of you, shame on you!

Jeremy just asked a very reasonable question about inviting guests and all you hooligans are embarrassing him."

The table talk settled down and Trey and Carol Sue secretly sent their love and excitement to each other with their eye contact. It was a wonderful gift for all of them to be together and to love each other with total devotion to each other's good.

Dinner finished, the girls helped clear the table and the young men headed for the stables to set up their horseshoe pitching court, which would invariably evolve into a rigorous, competitive contest. George and Renee sauntered out to the front porch and sat close to each other in the porch swing. Renee laid her head on George's shoulder as he put his arm around her. They just sat and soaked in each other's presence. Theirs was a deep and abiding love that served them well. Everyone around them benefited from their example. Life with the Smallwood-Casey clan never lacked for excitement or *love one to another.*

Joshua lingered to help the girls carry the dishes to the kitchen. Zoe blushed as she realized that he was particularly interested in helping her. This had been going on between them for several weeks now. It seemed one of them was forever appearing near the other's location. While others noticed, they were kind. Exchanged glances of *Did you see that? Isn't that something?* were the only communications in public. Margie and Jason had talked about it in the privacy of their bedroom and they were both pleased that this attraction was quite interesting and even beneficial to both Zoe and Joshua. Zoe was just fourteen and Joshua was about to turn twenty-two. The age difference was proper as long as they took it slowly.

The week passed rather quickly. Jeremy had to find an afternoon to journey over toward the Ashton parsonage. Margie suggested that he take a small gift for the church, noting its recovery. She found a lovely lace tablecloth that would be appropriate for the communion table. She created a card from the Casey/Smallwood Family to God's House of Worship, signed Brothers and Sisters in Christ. That was a wonderful excuse to show up on Alvina's doorstep and a really thoughtful idea. It worked. Reverend Ashton was very grateful for the gift of the altar cloth and he readily accepted the invitation for the next Sunday afternoon get together. It would be a big affair.

~ 14~

"All things work together for good to those who love the Lord and are called according to his purposes."
I Thessalonians 2:18

Martin and Rose's journey to Indiana was smooth and even enjoyable. The children were well behaved and everything went as planned. Travelling by train wasn't the most pleasant experience, but it certainly beat travelling by stage or wagon. Speeding along the countrywide was wonderful entertainment for the children, and Martin and Rose had more time together in those few days than they had had in months. The most difficult part of the trip was the distance and the hours being cooped up in a small space. That took a toll on all of them.

Martin's job was demanding. While he was training newly graduated doctors in the Army's standard operating procedure, he was also consulting with the President's cabinet. They were working out new protocol that involved the escalating need for medical attention in the reconstruction of the nation, as well as, adequate support for the troops and settlers in the newly evolving West. Going back and forth, from West Point to Washington, D.C., was tiring for Martin and time-consuming. His main mission was helping to develop curriculum that was succinct and beneficial for the Medical Corps that would be assigned to the newly emerging western territories.

While droves of settlers were pushing westward, the Army was solely responsible for their safety. It was an ever escalating problem as the Indians were pushed further and further out of their homelands.

It seemed the West and the South were in great need of assistance from the federal government. The census of 1870 recorded a population of almost thirty-nine million. It was a much lower increase than anticipated due mostly to the great loss of life in the Civil War. Interestingly enough the geographic center of America's population for the second decade in a row was in Ohio, just 48 miles northeast of Cincinnati, but droves of people were moving further westward.

The *Call of the West* meant new beginnings. Much of the land was free or at least very cheap and that provided for great opportunities for economic blessings and new beginnings. The problems were in the journey and particularly the threat of traveling through Indian Territories. While some tribes were often warlike most were not. The greatest problem was the invasion of their hunting grounds, which threatened their very existence. Adding to that threat, the meanness of many of the *intruders* caused them to become so aggressive.

An example of misspent and misplaced aggression by the Army was General George Custer's attack on a peaceful Indian village on November 27, 1868. The Seventh Calvary decimated this village which had migrated further north to find a peaceful and safe place to live. The Army had killed over one hundred warriors and almost eight hundred ponies, destroying large quantities of food and clothing. Instead of striking a blow against the hostiles, Custer had unwittingly killed one of the few Cheyenne leaders who were for peace.

Obviously, this kind of hostility was fueling the violence and increasing the danger for all that were involved. Martin's assignment was to encourage and support the medical outposts along the Overland Trail. George was thrilled to be included and was chompin' at the bit to gather the stories for publishing.

~ ~ ~

Saturday afternoon's passenger train from Cincinnati finally pulled into the station at Tampico, and the family was assembled to receive the entourage of The Martin Smallwoods with signs, flowers and happy, happy hearts. Baby Barton was extremely impressed with the "mocahotive." His mother had a firm hold on him. He wasn't afraid of anything. He thought the noise was all for his enjoyment.

Everyone was there except Jason and Trey. Someone had to mind the store. George and Renee were heading up the delegation. After all grandparents need to have some privileges. George spied Martin as he stepped into the stairwell to assist the children. Grandpa George rushed to help, hug and just weep a few tears of thanksgiving and gratitude. God had allowed, one more time, for father and son and grandchildren to be reunited. Well, actually, united for the first time with the little girls. Marilyn Rose was almost three and a half and Sally Renee had turned two just the month before. It would indeed be interesting to have two three-year-olds in the house counting Baby Barton, plus a tremendously active tiny girl and her older, and wiser, brother, Patrick.

Renee just broke down and wept at the sight of them and of course Rose was bringing up the rear, trying to hold on to Sally Renee who was whooping and hollering. She was kin to little Barton, nothing scared her. Actually, they were first cousins.

The midnight oil would burn tonight as months and the months of separation were sorted out. Everyone was on their best behavior, generally helping, arranging, taking care of the little ones and just catching up.

~ 15 ~

"Whoever gives to the poor will lack nothing,
but those who close their eyes to poverty
will be cursed."
Proverbs 28:27

George and Martin finally got some privacy after the evening meal that first night. They invited Jason to join them, but he declined knowing full well that they had big things to plan.

Martin began by describing the mission to his dad. George gave Martin his rapt attention and was soaking it in with total awe. It seemed that the general public was not aware of how bad things really were. Martin explained that the Army had been scaled down considerably since the Civil War. The western territory, where they were going, was approximately a third of the continental United States. It was nearly a million square miles. About fifteen thousand military personnel were pitted against more than three hundred thousand Indians. The Army was given the assignment of containing the peace, protecting the settlers and travelers, while of course taking care of themselves.

The saying which greeted each newly assigned soldier to the West was, "Save your last bullet for yourself. You don't want to be captured by the Indians." That was particularly true where there were roving bands of warriors that were definitely dedicated to revenge and victory.

"The politics involved," Martin explained, "were one of the biggest problems. Broken promises, treaty violations and just plain bad faith, especially on the part of the American government caused a lot more bloodshed than necessary."

"What can be done about that?" George asked.

"Probably nothing," Martin responded. "It's more serious than anyone could imagine. I've been on the edges of the controversy for several years now, and Washington only sees the government's side. My job is to help take care of the wounded with better planning and training for the Medical Corps who are assigned, particularly along the Overland Trail. Your job, Dad, is to be an observer, a journalist and an extra pair of eyes and ears – helping hands will be good too."

"I'll do my best, son." George quickly affirmed. "I assume anything I write for publication will have to be reviewed and censored if necessary."

"Yes, of course, that was a stringent requirement for your being able to accompany me. We will post your writings with the Department of the Army and publication will be forthcoming only as they release your work.

~ ~ ~

George "begged off" from church the next morning. He convinced Renee that he needed the time to gather information and begin research on everything he could find on the Overland Trail. The young Smallwood family was not ready to present themselves in public life either. The children were more tired than they or their mother realized. And, frankly, Rose was worn out. "Facilities" were not that readily available on trains and while they had a first-class compartment, still managing little ones had been a huge task.

George knew of the legislation that was pending in Washington. The name of the Bill was the "Indian Appropriations Act." Basically, it would end the policy of recognizing Indian tribes as sovereign nations and there would not be anymore negotiation through treaties. The act would make Indian policy through law and executive decision. Basically, the Indians would legally become wards of the nation. It was all coming to a head, but that was not decreasing the hostility and the need for more and more protection for the settlers moving west.

~ 16 ~

*"Look at those who are honest and good, for a
wonderful future awaits those who love peace."*
Psalm 37:37

The afternoon's activities kept the Casey home in a buzz.
Supper would have so many tones and undertones,
romances and sad thoughts of days of separation and even
danger to loved ones.

George and Martin were each preparing their own
minds and hearts, saying good-byes that would cover a
three months' absence. Everyone knew, without speaking of
it, that they would be in constant danger, yet it was a great
opportunity for father and son to be a part of history in the
making.

Rose and Renee were catching up for the lost time and
space of several years' separation. Renee holding and caring
for her grandchildren, whom she hadn't seen since Barton
Patrick was a newborn was a great delight and comfort. Not
to mention the little girls, who were more precious than life
itself warming up to Grandma Renee. "Bone of my bones,
flesh of my flesh," it was truly a spiritual reunion as well as
a physical one. Renee was overjoyed with the reunion and

torn with the thought of George and Martin leaving on their quest.

Zoe and Joshua were becoming more and more aware of each other, and truly Joshua's spiritual growth and change of mind had been almost a miracle of the century. Now, he was in a budding relationship with Zoe and she was heeding and feeding on his truthful and changed heart. It was so beautiful to observe as she was being "transformed by the renewing of her mind."

Trey and Carol Sue were ecstatic with the promise of their "growing" blessing. They were such wonderful young adults. They cared so much for so all those around them. They were a perfect match in so many ways. Their greatest attribute was their genuine maturity and acceptance of life and its trials, would that God remained close to them and their precious gift.

Margie's healing was ahead of all expectations and Jason's biggest job was keeping her from overdoing. Baby Barton Smallwood Casey was a handful, but Emma had really stepped up to lessen the load on her mother. Clayton and Abby were holding their own. Well, Clayton, didn't hold on to much, but in his quiet way at least he didn't cause any trouble. Abby was still the "bee charmer," and really never any trouble to anyone.

That left Jeremy and his highly charged self to entertain the Reverend and impress the Reverend's daughter. The Ashtons were to arrive mid-afternoon and the plot would thicken. Well, not actually a plot, but the posturing and the maneuvering would begin. Older generations, younger generation, new friends and acquaintances, all of it would be a very important part of life and its meanderings. It would be more than a normal Sunday evening gathering.

The party was "on." Twenty-one folks, counting Tammy, and she was always counted, made twenty-two. Tables were set outside under the big trees and festivity was the order of the day.

Jeremy anxiously watched for Reverend Ashton and Alvina to appear. He didn't want to seem *anxious*, but there wasn't much he could do to curtail his excitement. *There they were!* He had just come through the front door, as he scanned the road in front of the house, for the fifteenth time in the past hour. *Oh! My!* Alvina looked beautiful. She was beautiful! She had a lovely parasol shading her even lovelier bonnet of yellow straw with blue trim. A matching blue dress was just the compliment she needed to her lovely blonde hair. Jeremy's breath caught in his throat. Who would ever have known that "love" could make one short of breath, even short of air to breathe. He knew he was in love with Alvina. He knew because he had never before felt as he felt now - - heady, nervous and totally speechless.

"Good afternoon, Ashen Reverton," Jeremy tried to make his mouth and frozen brain function as he stepped up to Alvina's side of the wagon. "I mean, Reverend Ashton," he half muttered as he felt the blood rush to his face. "I'm so glad you and Alvina could come this afternoon. We're honored to have you."

Margie had been watching too. She was already outside. Jason had helped her negotiate the front porch steps and she was moving along nicely, one good leg and one good arm got her where she wanted to go. She came up behind Jeremy just in time to bring a semblance of decorum and ease to the greeting. "Hello . . . and welcome to the Casey Circus. So glad you could join us today. It's a special occasion with my brother and his wife and children visiting and the eminent departure of my father and brother to the *unknown dangers of the West*." Margie was a bit dramatic, but it was indeed a big day, not to mention the introduction of Jeremy's newly declared, beloved Alvina.

Reverend Ashton secured the reins of his team and went around the wagon to assist Alvina's descent. Too late . . . Jeremy had already accomplished that delightful task and fled, with Alvina on his arm, halfway across the yard by the time the Reverend brushed himself off and tipped his hat to Margie. "Well, Mrs. Casey, we are certainly glad to be invited to such a fine gathering. I trust you are all having a blessed Sunday."

Margie assured him of their *blessedness* on this fine Sunday afternoon and guided him across the lawn where she saw Jason and George chatting away as they rested on the front porch.

Jeremy and Alvina had joined the other young people around on the side porch. They were sipping lemonade and having a cheerful conversation. Jeremy rather bounced up the steps as he announced, "Well, everybody, I want you to meet Alvina Ashton." Jeremy continued with a polite but excited voice. "Let's see, Alvina, you know my brother Trey, uhhhh this is his wife Carol Sue." Taking Alvina by the arm, he made a half-circle introducing Joshua and Zoe, Jacob and Emma.

Four young couples, one married, two courting and one comprised of two individuals, Jacob and Emma, ready to brave the world as individuals, somewhat prepared but still in the bud of life. Oh, how the scene had changed from the day that the Wilson children first landed at the Casey homestead. It had been almost twelve years ago and time had certainly matured this batch of young Americans. It truly was a delightful sight to behold.

Alvina offered her "hellos" and there were handshakes all around. Trey was the first to speak, which Jeremy dreaded, but Trey was very considerate. "Well, Alvina, it is wonderful to have you and your father with us this afternoon. We were just talking about how much we enjoy these get-to-gathers on Sundays."

"I am overwhelmed," Alvina responded, really almost embarrassing herself. She continued, "I can't imagine having . . . how many, eight brothers and sisters. I've been alone all of my life. I'm an only child."

"Uh, oh," Jacob quipped, "does that mean you're spoiled, Alvina?"

Everyone chuckled politely, as Jeremy took up Alvina's cause, "Well, she keeps house for her father, cooking, cleaning, doing the laundry and takes care of the church. I wouldn't say that's spoiled."

"Just kidding, Brother, I just can't imagine being an only child, although, there are times I try to imagine it," Jacob explained and amused everyone as usual.

They all chuckled as they turned to their various conversations and attentions. Zoe and Joshua very much interested only in each other, which was noticed by everyone. It was also obvious that Jeremy and Alvina had eyes for only each other. Jacob remarked to Emma how disgusting it was to see all the "love birds" fluttering about. Emma laughed out loud and then caught herself – not wanting to share the remark or the reason for the laugh.

~ ~ ~

The rest of the afternoon and evening was very pleasant. It was indeed a wonderful gathering of family and almost family. Martin and Rose were busy with the little folks, but Grandmother Renee was always lending a hand, something Rose had not been accustomed to since they lived so far from home. It was really nice and very helpful. It would be especially helpful with Martin and George gone for so long.

~ 17 ~

*"The eternal God is your refuge, and his
everlasting arms are under you."*
Deuteronomy 33:27

George and Martin were scheduled to meet the main
body assigned to Martin's expedition to the west in
just two weeks. The "jumping off" place was Fort Leavenworth, Kansas, one of the older military establishments
of the American government. It was founded in the early
1800's and was the farthest western fort. It was located only
ten miles north of the 18th century French Fort de Cavagnal,
an outpost of the Louisiana Territory. Fort Leavenworth had
seen many early American explorers on the Missouri River
including Lewis and Clark in 1804. In the early development
of the west, the soldiers of Fort Leavenworth were the main
protection of the Sante Fe Trail travelers.

When the Civil War began, Camp Lincoln was established at Fort Leavenworth as a training station for the Union
Army, mainly to train the Kansas volunteers. The Army's
chief mission in maintaining Fort Leavenworth was to control the Indian tribes on the Western plains. The Indian Wars
were a constant mission of the fort to train and dispatch
troops across the western territories. The Apache, Modoc,

Cheyenne, Comanche, Kiowa, Kickapoo and the Nez Perces were the main tribes, among the many, who were constantly either attacking or defending themselves from the huge tide of pioneers, hunters, gold miners, land speculators, basically all invaders of the once closely held lands of the American Indian.

The Army was spread thin and the casualties were a great risk and a burden to the stability of the troops of the West. Martin was hopeful that his training and experience could somehow improve the medical care *in place* or the *lack* there of. Doctors were a premium in the whole of the nation. The maintaining of health and home, body and soul, so far away from civilization was as tremendous task.

The Overland Stage route continued to encounter problems with the Indians resulting in many emigrants killed and hundreds of horses and mules run off. Ranches along the South Platte River were attacked, with men killed and women and children taken prisoner. Livestock was stolen and the ranch buildings were burned. The telegraph lines were forever being destroyed and communication was impaired if it existed at all. Even the railroad lines were destroyed and ravaged by the continuing battle of the Indians to defend their land.

George and Martin were excited and saddened. Probably more excited, however, as it was the call of the "wild and woolly west," and they were going to be in the big middle of it. Their plan was to leave Monday morning aboard the train from Tampico headed for Kansas City. Through the various railroad lines and transfers, they should arrive at Fort Leavenworth within twenty-four hours. The medical detachment would assemble there and the whole contingency would travel by train as far as Denver. From there they would begin their march westward as they stopped at the appointed stations along the Overland Trail to inspect and recommend what needed to be done to assist these outposts.

~ 18 ~

*"Do not despise these small beginnings,
for the LORD rejoices to see the work begin."*
Zechariah 4:10

The Sunday afternoon gathering was coming to an end, and the Ashtons were saying their good-byes and *thank-yous*. Jeremy was fraught to tell Alvina good-bye. When would he see her again? He had found time after the picnic to stroll with her in private and tell her, in his halting way, how he felt about her. "Alvina, I don't really know how to say this. I've never said anything like this before."

"Well, Jeremy, I have probably never heard anything like . . . uhhhh what you're going to say before." Alvina laughed nervously and turned away just slightly.

Jeremy, stepped into her space and put his hands on her shoulders. She turned to look straight into his deep, blue eyes, the moment was magic. He wanted to kiss her, but he didn't quite feel that brave. Instead, he winked at her and she laughed again. "Oh, Alvina, if only I had the words to tell you what you mean to me. I didn't know such feelings existed." He paused to read her expression and was one of anticipation. It was as though she was saying, *"Don't stop there, Jeremy."*

He didn't. "Alvina, I don't want to frighten you with my forwardness, but I have to know if you feel the same toward me. If you do, then I want to give you this ring, that was my mother's. It doesn't have to be an engagement ring – but just a "hold in place" until we can get this done properly. I guess I'm saying . . . I'm promising you that I intend to pursue our friendship, or courtship, or whatever you want to call it. Will you accept it as a promise?"

She nodded her yes and accepted the ring, but she told him that she thought better of wearing it just now. She explained that she needed to have enough respectable space for courting that would please her father's finer opinions. Jeremy stole a sweet kiss and they rushed back to be among the folks.

Joshua and Zoe had found time to steal a visit as well. Joshua realized that he definitely had feelings for Zoe, but he wasn't sure how she felt. It was a bit awkward since they were somewhat related. Well, not cousins or anything, really not blood relatives at all, but they had grown up in the same family. They shared the same parents. Well, not exactly the same. Margie was Joshua's stepmother and his father, Jason was Zoe's stepfather. And, the fact that Joshua was eight years older than Zoe caused him to err on the side of caution and responsibility toward Zoe. Mean while, Joshua wasn't the only one that realized something was developing between them.

Trey and Carol Sue had been close to them both since the beginning of summer and realized the "signs" were there. They always seemed to end up in the same places at the same time with casual flirtations going both directions and the most obvious thing of all was the melting of Zoe's heart. You could read it like a book. She was so very kind and attentive to Joshua. Really, that was almost out of character for Zoe. Kindness and being attentive to anyone other than herself were traits that had been missing in her entire life to this point.

~ ~ ~

Margie encouraged Martin and Rose to go for a buggy ride a little later that evening. She assured them that between her and Tammy, Emma, Abby and Zoe they could maintain the Smallwood little people. They were more than willing to take her up on her offer. There wasn't much privacy around the Casey household and especially if Marilyn Rose and Sally Renee could find them.

George and Renee had left earlier and were planning to spend their last evening together with some serious talk, lots of laughter and most of all just sharing their love and devotion for the time to come. In fact Renee had some wifely instructions for George mostly regarding his taking care of himself and coming home to her.

As they enjoyed a cup of tea on the front porch Renee set her cup down and put her arms around George's neck to tell him, "George, Honey, you cannot leave me now. I don't mean leave to go on this soiree with Martin, I mean you cannot leave my life as my husband. I am very accustomed to having you around and it's been the best thing that ever happened to me."

"Awwww, Renee, you don't need to worry. We'll be fine. We're just going to do some poking around out west and Martin will do some teaching, I'll do some writing – and we'll be home before you know it."

"Yes, Sir George, I know about that poking around you men do. You'll be in the big middle of the first battle you can find - and then some. I'm just telling you – you have to take care of yourself for me! I need you! I can't live without you! Or, at least I don't want to."

With that last outburst, George planted a big, fat kiss smack on Renee's mouth and that closed her mouth for awhile.

~ 19 ~

"There will always be poor people in the land. Therefore I command you to be open handed toward your brothers and toward the poor and needy in your land."
Deuteronomy 15:11

~ Fall of 1872 ~

George and Martin had been ordered to accompany troops headed for Fort Hartsuff in Nebraska. There had been a great many confrontations between the Sioux Indians and the settlers. George's mission of training the Medical Corps along the Overland Trail had not lasted more than a few weeks. The only thing that exceeded the number of attacks and skirmishes with the Indians was the confusion. Confusion was rampant among the military commands. When a commanding officer realized that Martin was a doctor on the loose, his orders changed immediately.

The best thing that George had been able to do was issue a printed directive that he had brought with him to distribute to the troops. Basically it was a "To Do List:"

"Take Care of Your Health"

Sickness disables or destroys three times as many of our soldiers as does the enemy.

Sunstroke may be prevented by wearing a handkerchief in the crown of the hat. It is better to keep it moist. If you don't have a handkerchief, use wet grass. If drinking water is scarce, at least you must rinse your mouth with just a small swallow of water every few hours.

Experience teaches old soldiers that the less they drink on a march the better. You will suffer less in the end by controlling your desire to drink large amounts, however urgent. Never eat heartily just before a great undertaking, because the nervous power is irresistibly drawn to the stomach to manage the food eaten. Eating too much will drain off the blood supply you need for the brain and muscles to function efficiently.

The sound of men on the march was a sound that Martin and George well remembered. It reminded them both of the days and nights they had endured during the Civil War. The War between the north and the south had been fought on home ground, so to speak. There were cities and towns, roads and railroads. Supply wagons and trains coming and going and simply put, civilization surrounded them. This was different. The wide open spaces were lonely and filled with the "men of the land," not these interlopers, these uniformed soldiers.

Many of the troops assigned to the western outposts were young and inexperienced. Their struggle to stay alive was not just facing the enemy, but *facing* themselves and their own basic daily needs. Along with the sheer physical suffering in the field, the soldiers bore the psychological burden of knowing that they were on their own. Help was never near them in that vast, unsettled country. It didn't take any of them long to realize that the difference between life and death, was their ability to survive, some way or another. They hardly ever knew where they were going, and except in the smallest units, even less of what they were doing.

The Indians, on the other hand, knew the terrain, usually had their families nearby or at least reachable. They could live on nothing and were used to creating all that they needed. Their weapons did not measure up to that of the Army – but they were on home ground – and could manage much longer and stronger.

George's writings were filled with human interest angles. He interviewed the soldiers and did his best to encourage and support them. They were so young and so far from home. The older men were not so willing to talk, hardened by years of fighting and surviving. They did what was expected of them and just moved through the days and nights of hardship.

Martin was trying to maintain some semblance of his original mission, and the mission he had been sent on was to train medical personnel. He had managed to salvage a small group to accompany him from post to post and was visiting the settlements, mostly rest stops along the way on the trails west.

The small entourage that had accompanied Martin had just saddled up and left Fort Hartsuff. There were fifteen of them, counting George and Martin. There was a Lieutenant and a Sergeant. They were several hours out on the trail and it was nearing noon.

Their destination was a full day's ride from the Fort. It was a modified and enlarged rest station where a number of infantrymen were assigned with a sergeant in charge. They were there to protect the station and the travelers. A small company of soldiers made a daily swoop around a five-mile

BMI Ministry Correspondence

❖

"Now here is my greeting which I am writing with my own hand, as I do at the end of all my letters, for proof that it really is from me. This is my own handwriting." -II Thessalonians 3:17

Thank you for being a part of this great of this harvest of souls.

-Sarah

radius of the station. It was routine. Nothing was happening to indicate any enemy activity.

It was nearing midday as George and Martin were on what they thought was a routine ride. The sun was almost directly overhead. They really didn't know what hit them. George was riding toward the back of the small group and wasn't paying much attention to anything. In fact, he was thinking and creating what he wanted to write that evening when they settled down at their destination.

The first indication of an attack was a loud and wild whooping, almost a screaming that was a loud blood-curdling sound. Then the front and back of the column was hit simultaneously.

The Indians were firing at a rapid pace and by the time the soldiers readied their weapons at least five of them were shot. It was fast and furious. Martin had been riding midway in the troop and reacted quickly. His horse reared but he was able to control his mount and he whirled to the right away from the attack and managed to head toward a small stand of trees near a gully. Sergeant Seaton was shouting commands and five of the troopers wheeled around to follow him. They made it to the gully where they dismounted and began firing at the attacking band of marauders. Martin didn't have time to locate his father, but he realized that if action wasn't taken immediately all would be lost.

George was wounded and fell from his horse. He didn't even have a weapon so he lay perfectly still as though he were dead. The attackers continued to pursue the few soldiers that were left as they bolted through the attack at the front and rode at the command of the lieutenant toward the other side of the trail.

There were only nine of the wandering band who ambushed the military column, but they were well prepared and springing such an unexpected surprise were very much on the winning side. One of the troopers had managed to get off a shot and had brought down one of the Indians. Another had his horse shot out from under him and he was a foot trying to avoid the firing from the soldiers who were able to fire back into those attacking.

Martin saw his father lying by the side of the road and assumed the worst. The rest of the attackers were hot on the heels of the fleeing soldiers riding away from the scene. Martin ordered the four soldiers with him to cover him as he bolted into the open to see about his dad.

By this time, George had chanced a look at what was taking place. He had been shot in the back, and his pain had turned from numbness to a severe throbbing. Martin dismounted on the run and crouched at his father's side. He was relieved to see his father moving. The wound was very obvious as the blood was pouring forth and the ground was saturated around him.

"Dad, dad," Martin called out, "hang on. I've got you. Where are you hit?"

"Don't know . . ." George struggled to catch his breath as he managed to roll to his side.

"I played dead . . . couldn't fight back, no gun . . . just guts!"

"Well, your guts are not in very good shape now." As Martin ripped George's shirt apart to see what was going on, the surviving four arrived at the scene.

"It looks like we're in the clear for now," the sergeant addressed Martin. He knew he had disobeyed orders to keep their position, but he saw the disappearing cloud of dust as the pursuers chased off after the others. Sergeant Seaton decided to assist Colonel Smallwood.

"Yes, yes," Martin replied, "send a man on up the road to see what's going on. I need to move this man, but first, hand me my saddle bags. I need to pack this wound and stop the blood flow before we can move him."

Martin was able to bandage George enough to control the bleeding and realized that the bullet had entered to the side of his spine and had gone through the flesh. There was an exit wound on the front of his left side and it didn't appear that any other damage had occurred.

~ 20 ~

"This is what the LORD says: Stop at the crossroads and look around. ask for the old, godly way, and walk in it. Travel its path, and you will find rest for your souls."
Jeremiah 6:16

B ack home, the fall term of school had begun. Joshua was back in Bloomington at Indiana University. This would be his last year. Jacob had gone off to pursue his heart's desire at Indiana Normal Teacher's College. His love for life and learning could not be contained. He would make an excellent teacher and his personality only served to enhance his abilities. This program was only two years and Jacob would be a full-fledged, educated teacher by the time he would turn twenty.

Margie's health had improved in the last thirty days and she was almost back to normal. She had pain in her leg, but she managed to do her share of the household work and the happiest of all was Baby Barton. He had been very patient waiting for his mommy to be his "mommy" once again. Jason's tender, loving attention had been a big factor in her healing and of course Renee was the "best" when it came to nursing and quality care.

Getting Joshua and Jacob off to school hadn't been any small task. Emma and Zoe were lonely and spent a lot of time together just talking and thinking about the boys, wondering what they were doing. Emma was taking her place alongside Miss Persinger as a teacher's helper and Zoe had one more year to complete her schooling and graduate a full-fledged, educated young lady of the day.

Margie was in the kitchen helping Tammy do the last of the canning. The fall apples and the last of the berries had been harvested and they were up to their elbows in jam, jellies and canned apples. Tom Barkman, knocked at the back door as Margie hurried to grab a tea towel and wipe her hands. She knew as soon as she saw Tom that there was some important news. Everybody in Tampico knew when they saw Tom coming that a telegram was being delivered. There weren't that many telegrams, and they hardly ever brought good news.

This one didn't either. It was from Martin and he was telling of the ambush and George's condition. It was sketchy but informative.

Dad wounded Indian attack. Faring well. Delayed in our return. More later.

Tell Rose and Renee. Don't worry. Love Martin

George and Martin were expected back around the middle of September and since it wasn't yet time the family hadn't worried about them. Letters came every now and then and they were always interesting as George unwound the saga of the west. Margie's first words to Tammy as she read were, "I knew things were going too well. We're spread from *heaven to breakfast*, as Aunt Stella used to say. Boys are in school so far from home. Martin and Dad in the west being attacked by Indians, and the girls are weeping around not knowing what to do with themselves. Jason is so busy he meets himself coming and going, and I'm up to my neck in apples and blackberries." She left Abby, Jeremy and Clay out of her inventory. There were just too many of them to be concerned about all of them all of the time.

With that little tirade, she was taking off her apron and moving toward the back porch to check on Baby Barton and then over to Renee's to find Rose and the children. Rose had been staying with her mother since Martin and George had left on their western adventures. Margie scooped Barton up from the floor and handed him to Tammy. That was a ritual that she had developed with whomever she left the baby. When she handed him off, it meant, "he's yours now." She hurried, as quickly as she could and harnessed Sugar to her little cart. Abby, Zoe and Clayton were in school, so everyone was accounted for – except to deliver the news of her dad's misfortune to Renee.

As she pulled up in front of Renee and George's little house she saw Rose in the backyard hanging out clothes. Rose saw her and waved as she rescued Sally Renee from the rain barrel. Actually, she wasn't in the rain barrel, but she was teetering on the side of the porch next to it. One more second and she would be in it. It was nearly impossible to keep that little girl in tow. She should have been named after Barton, her daddy's twin brother. He was never where he was supposed to be, doing what he should be doing. Really, that was the unfortunate cause of his accidental death. He never stopped to think of the consequences.

By the time Rose gathered up Sally, Margie had come around the side of the house. Marilyn Rose had spied her Auntie Margie and had engaged her in a nice conversation. You could always expect to have a nice conversation with Marilyn. She was so grown up and polite.

"What are you doing running around the countryside, Miss Margie?" Rose was in a good mood even though she was constantly on duty with three children under five.

"Well, I got a telegram from Martin. It's about Dad. He's injured. The message seems to say he is alright, but their return home will be delayed. He asked me to tell you and your mother. Here, Rose . . . here's the telegram," Margie handed it to Rose.

"Oh, my!" Rose covered her mouth with her hand as she managed to set Sally down on the back step. "Are you sure your father is all right?"

"Well, Martin said not to worry."

"He always says that, Margie, you know him he's the calmest person I've ever known."

"Where is your mother, Rose? I need to tell her."

"She's with Doctor Cummings, wherever they are this morning. Let's see, it's Wednesday. They're usually in the office on Wednesday mornings."

"Well, are you alright? I mean can I go on and find her?" Margie asked Rose, taking special care to observe her behavior and responses.

"Yes, yes . . . I'm fine, please go ahead. I would offer to go with you, but taking four of us anyplace is always a chore."

"Thank you, Rose, I can find her and she will probably be on home as soon as she can. If I take Marilyn Renee with me . . . will that help you?"

"Oh, yes, thank you . . . Patrick is here, some place." And, there he was. He had heard Aunt Margie talking with his mother and he had appeared in the middle of their conversation. Neither one of the women noticed him. He was a little gentleman and always very considerate of the grownups. Patrick and Marilyn seemed to makeup somewhat for Sally's behavior – there is a God.

Margie and Marilyn climbed in the little buggy and headed toward the center of town. Margie was hoping that Jason was at the store, and she could stop and see him. She wanted him to know about her father. He was always such a comfort and knew just what needed to be done.

As she turned down the alley toward the back of the store, she saw Jason coming out the back door.

"Margie and Marilyn, what are you two ladies doing on this beautiful fall day? "

"Oh, Jason, Honey," calming herself so that she wouldn't upset Marilyn, she waited for Jason to come to her. "I just got a telegram from Martin that Dad has been injured. They were attacked by Indians and Martin managed to get a telegram off to us. I'm on my way to find Renee."

"She's at Doc Cummings, Honey. I saw her just a few minutes ago. She was in the store. They needed some rubbing alcohol. . . but, what about your father? Is he okay . . . I mean what's the extent of his injuries?"

"I don't know. The telegram doesn't say much. Here read it. I just need you to go with us. I'm sure Renee will be fine. She always takes everything in stride, but I know she's been through so much and you are always such a calming influence."

With that Marilyn had climbed out of the cart and was holding Jason's hand. Margie grabbed her shawl and joined Jason and Marilyn as they all three walked down the alley toward Doctor Cumming's office.

Renee was in the front office and when she saw the three of them, she knew something must be wrong. "Margie, Jason, what brings you here . . . what's wrong. Is Rose all right? Is it Patrick or Sally . . . what's going on?"

It was not like Renee to panic. Actually, she wasn't panicking, but she was not her calm and collected self.

"Oh, Renee, it's George and he's alive. He's injured. Martin has sent me a telegram, and I came to tell you and Rose."

"How badly is he injured?"

"We don't know. Here read the telegram for yourself. Martin said not to worry. Really, he was just telling us about the . . . uhhhh . . . incident and that their return would be delayed some."

Margie handed Renee the telegram as Renee sank into the nearest chair. "Grandmother, are you all right?" Marilyn hurried to her side.

"Oh, yes, Honey, Grandmother is fine. I'm just a little surprised that's all."

Renee had regained her usual composure and realized that she needed to be calm and sensible. "Where has this telegram come from?" Renee asked as she continued, "The envelope says it's a military wire and it doesn't indicate its origin. I know they were at Fort Hartsuff in Nebraska according to the last letter I got from George," Renee offered.

"To tell you the truth, Renee, I haven't kept up with their travels. I just figured you and Rose were doing all that . . . I'm sure we can find out," Margie was taking charge now.

Jason joined in the conversation with some good words of being patient for now and waiting for more news. Jason had been praying and invoking God's presence among them all as they stood their ground and turned their faith quotient up. They all knew that their lives were in God's hands and that He was sufficient for all their needs.

Jason continued, "Renee, we have to think the best and holdout for the good news of George's mending and return to us. This is a shock and while we might have wondered about their safety, we didn't expect anything to happen to either one of them. Martin is with him and that's the best medical attention he could have."

Renee shook her head in agreement as she reached in her apron pocket to retrieve her hanky. She wiped her eyes and blew her nose and stood up to hug Margie. "Oh, Margie, I'm so sorry . . . and so thoughtless. My goodness we're not only worrying about my husband, but I should have thought of you. You've had George longer than I have . . . and . . . with a big gust of courage . . . we're just going to believe as Jason has said, that God is in charge and this too shall pass."

With that little speech, Renee turned and said, "I've got to get back to work. The good doctor will think I ran off and joined the circus. I'll stop by your place on my way home. Is Rose okay?"

"Yes, she's fine, Renee. I just brought Miss Marilyn along to give Rose some help. Of course, if I really wanted to help her, I should have brought Miss Sally."

With that confession, they all laughed a light and airy laugh and the women hugged each other knowing that they were going to meet the need of the hour . . . they always did. *"If God be for you – who could be against you?"*

~ ~ ~

A thousand miles away, George was resting comfortably and Martin was managing the recovery. The soldiers at the head of their little convoy had outrun the Indians and made it to the rest station. The racquet of the racing survivors brought out the reserves, garroted at the station.

The sergeant in charge shouted the orders to saddle up and charge to assist. A few troops had just returned from their morning rounds.

"Hostiles! Prepare for defense!" the sergeant shouted. And, defend they did! The pursuing Indians didn't know what was happening. Suddenly, bullets were flying all around them and they quickly cut off their chase and disappeared into the brush.

The mounted troops from the station pursued for a short distance and were called off by the retreat bugle. A contingency of rescuers mustered and returned to the scene of the attack. They had brought a wagon and therefore George could be transported to the settlement. His bleeding had stopped and Martin had employed his best doctoring skills, disinfecting the wound and dressing his side after a few stitches to close the wound. If infection was staid – George would fully recover. He was very lucky or was it blessed? He wasn't a young man, but he was a tough one. Two of their troops had not been so lucky and it was a sad letter that went to the families of those fallen soldiers

~ 21 ~

"Don't be afraid, for I am with you. Don't be discouraged, for I am your God. I will strengthen you and help you. I will hold you up with my victorious right hand."
Isaiah 41:10

Life had settled down to some extent back in Tampico. Renee and Rose were as satisfied as they could possibly be over George's recovery. Martin had gotten a letter off to Rose and George had managed to scribble a few lines to Renee. The women were holding their own and were prayerfully awaiting the welcome return of the men.

George had been able to write several really good, newsworthy stories before the fateful day. Describing the conditions and interviewing the soldiers proved to be an interesting unfolding of the mystery of the great West. The one story that he was most pleased with dealt with the great Indian Peace Council. It took place in 1840 according to the white man's telling. However, the Indians' way of counting time referred to it as "seven winters since the great shower of meteors." They had marked time and named it the "Winter the Stars Fell."

An older Indian man who lived with the soldiers and the settlers at the outpost could speak enough English to converse with George. During George's convalescing, he worked through the conversations and stories from what some of the soldiers had also collected, to write an account of the great gathering. While the numbers were really unknown, it was for sure that the numbers were huge. All the tribes had been called together to council and decide what the future held for them as the white invaders continued to come.

George wrote. *Men and women, boys and girls traveled from north and south over hundreds of miles of treeless grasslands toward their selected meeting ground on a river that had once been a kind of boundary between the enemy tribes. They met at a river they called Flint Arrowpoint near Bent's Trading House. The white traders called it the Arkansas River. The Cheyenne and Arapaho tribes arrived first on the north bank of the river.*

George's story continued to unfold. *The Cheyenne, the Arapaho, the Kiowas and some of their Comanche allies had come from the north as far as six hundred miles away. Meeting with once-deadly enemies, caused every man to be on guard, eyeing each other with guarded apprehension.*

As the stories, and embellishments of stories continued, George gathered many interesting facts, including the richness of the Kiowa and the Comanche due to their horse herds. *The old Indian man may have been exaggerating, but he reckoned that there were as many as 8,000 horses. He recounted how as a boy he had scrambled up a tree when they heard the thundering herds coming. He told how they called back and forth, "I see them coming! Yes! Out there!"*

"How many?" someone cried. "Eeeeee! There are many! I see the dust clouds covering the sky." As the sound grew louder and louder, they felt the earth trembling as the hoof beats pounded the earth. The newcomers were bringing more horses than had ever been seen or dreamed of.

George's stories were fascinating – the readers back East would hang on every word. His biggest regret was that he had been injured and was considerably handicapped in his journalistic efforts.

If you had asked Renee and Rose they would have told you they really were far more interested in his and Martin's safe return. The Indians were someplace else and the women had plans for family and future nearer home.

~ ~ ~

Thanksgiving was fast approaching and the hope that was discussed concerned Martin and George's return to the safety of the family by Thanksgiving. The college folks, Joshua and Jacob, would be home and the girls were in a dither, decorating, baking, sewing and being just plain excited. Emma enjoyed and longed for the family gatherings for the pure and simple reason that she loved the "family." Zoe had a special "love." It happened to be a certain young man. Never mind that he had been under the same roof for the past ten or so years. Zoe and Josh had begun to notice each other last summer. Josh had been a godsend to her then as she struggled through some growing up situations and his attention had turned to become romantic in nature. He had written to her faithfully throughout the fall semester.

Trey and Carol Sue were enjoying the excitement of becoming parents after the first of the year and Jeremy was in love. He and Alvina had "kept company" and, they were headed for a spring wedding. That is, providing Alvina's father gave his permission. The prospects were very good.

Alvina spent as much time as possible in Tampico, visiting with Carol Sue. If the girls happened to need to go down to Clay's Emporium, they just might run into Trey and Jeremy. Any excuse would do to make the trip and the visit to the store. Alvina usually came on some trumped-up errand

and wasn't fooling anybody. Her friend, Ruthie, accompanied her or Alvina's father would not have allowed her to be on the road that far. He knew what was going on and secretly was very pleased.

Jeremy had already asked Rev. Ashton for Alvina's hand and Jeremy was about to burst waiting until Thanksgiving and the family gathering to pop the question. Rev. Ashton agreed to keep it a secret. In fact, he had suggested that Jeremy give Alvina her mother's keepsake ring when he asked her to marry him. It was all too perfect. It would be the highlight of Thanksgiving. Well, if only Martin and George returned by Thanksgiving, it would be the perfect family gathering.

As preparations continued . . . "Tom Turkey" was getting fatter by the day. Barton thought the turkey belonged to him since his mother let him feed it every day. Margie began to worry about what she was going to tell Barton when Tom disappeared. She had already warned Zoe, Clay, Abby and Emma to please be careful and not give it away. That is - that Tom would be the featured guest at the Thanksgiving table.

Jason was busier than usual. The store was bustling. He had taken on some new items making Casey's Emporium one of the most up-to-date clothiers in the whole southern part of the state. Styles had evolved in the recent years during the recovery of the Civil War, and Jason was an astute business man. He didn't overstock. He just brought enough to give the local folks an idea of what was available. He did a land office catalogue business.

Zoe was doing so well in school and in every other area of life. She had become a regular in the church choir and Pastor Robertson was always and forever commenting to Margie how pleased he was with Zoe's new self. Margie just gave thanks to God and privately, hopefully watched over all her children. Margie knew that Zoe and Josh were becoming quite an item in the romance department, and she talked with

Jason in the privacy of their time together. He encouraged her to just "hide and watch."

"After all, Margie Dear, God has brought this family together for the good of all . . . and we just need to put our trust in Him."

"I know, I know, Jason, it's just that I worry. Emma and Abby have exceeded my fondest expectations. They are growing into lovely young ladies and Zoe seems to have changed. I just hope that she and Joshua are headed in the right direction and it works out the best for both of them."

~ ~ ~

Last minute details were being attended to all day on Wednesday. The family was planning to attend the Thanksgiving Vesper services that evening. Pastor Robertson had established a special service for the community to gather together to give thanks as the Body of Christ. The Methodists and the Baptists had set the example and had been alternating churches each year to host the service.

The singing had just commenced at the opening of the service when two weary, very happy men entered the vestibule at the back of the church. George and Martin spied their family all lined up. They filled two pews with the seventeen members of that loving family who were present and accounted for. Rose and Renee were next to the wall about halfway down the left side. George and Martin quietly slipped down the side aisle and Rose nearly let out a gladsome cry when she realized Martin had slipped in beside her and the children.

Renee gasped as George put his arm around her waist and she stopped singing just so she could catch her breath. Tears spilled down her cheeks as she gazed into George's tired, green eyes. Waves of thanksgiving and more tears accompanied her voice as she found her place and continued to sing:

We gather together to ask the Lord's blessing;
He chastens and hastens His will to make known.
The wicked oppressing now cease from distressing -
Sing praises to His name, He forgets not His own.

Renee's voice rose as she thought of what she was singing, "Praises to His name." Her husband and life mate had been returned to her. It was time to "cease from distressing." George had come back to her. He looked pale and worn, but he was alive.

Margie turned to see if the moving and scuffling was owing to any of her brood and she grinned from ear to ear as she gently nudged Jason and nodded her head toward the newly arrived surprises. Thanksgiving could soar to the heavens now and forever. They were all present and accounted for once again.

~ ~ ~

The dinner was outstanding, as expected. There seemed to be enough food to feed an army, but then really the Casey/Wilson/Smallwood clan was a small army. It was a toss-up as to which table was having the most fun. The grown-ups were ecstatic with their complete cadre of husband and wives. Only Rev. Ashton was alone, but he joined right in, as pastors do. Everyone extended extra effort to include him.

The children were bubbling over with the excitement of the grand dinner and all the wonderful goodies. Barton was a little suspicious about the big bird in front of his father's place at the grown-up's table. And, he hadn't seen Tom since yesterday evening. He didn't say anything or ask any questions. It was all going well. Margie was keeping an eye on him.

The talk was filled with George and Martin's exciting escapades. George tried to play it down and really out of character, Martin played it up.

"I'm telling you, I thought we were goners when those Indians swooped down on us. The men were stellar in their bravery. I began to flash back to the many battles I witnessed in the War. But, then you really don't have time to think when you're trying to stay mounted and alive. When I saw Dad go down, I lost my concentration for awhile, but a young soldier next to me was bravely challenging all comers and I realize I had to respond too."

Joshua was particularly interested in all the details and struck up a conversation with Martin, who was sitting by his side. Although, Joshua had just narrowly escaped soldiering in the Civil War, he had a deep and abiding desire to know and understand the thoughts and feelings of men in battle. His "call" was becoming more and more evident as he was nearing the completion of his education. He sought out Rev. Ashton at the close of the meal to talk about "pastoring." It wasn't to be a surprise to any of the family. They had known and seen Joshua's heart for the Lord and his people. After all, Zoe was a homegrown product of transformation under the friendship and love of a brother in Christ. Josh had proven himself. He would make a wonderful pastor.

Martin, Rose and the children prepared to leave to go back to West Point within the week following Thanksgiving. It would be a lonely time for Renee and the whole family really. Barton was always begging to go play with Patrick and his sisters. Barton tried to boss them all around. He did fairly well with that except for Baby Sally. She had a mind of her own. I wonder where she got that. Could be that Grandmother Renee was reincarnated in that little filly. "Determination" and "Grit" were her middle names.

~ 22 ~

"Those who obey God's commandments remain in fellowship with him, and he with them. And we know he lives in us because the Spirit he gave us lives in us."
I John 3:24

C hristmas came and went with much celebration and gift giving. Life was good and time moving on. Carol Sue and Trey were counting the days, waiting for the birth of the third generation of their family. Carol Sue spent a lot of time with Margie. Just being near her was a comfort. She enjoyed helping with Barton.

"Margie, I don't know how you do it all," Carol Sue commented as she witnessed Margie's constant and ever-loving presence day-by-day.

"It isn't so hard, Carol Sue. When you're taking care of the people you love, it's the greatest joy of life. I just thank God everyday for health and order. Well, at least some semblance of order."

"Oh, I'd say there's lots of order. I think about my mother a lot as I watch you. She would have loved being in the middle of all the comings and goings of this family. I feel so bad about her life. It was so hard. After my father died, she struggled so to keep me and my brother going. When he left, it nearly broke her heart. In fact, I think she died of a broken heart." Carol Sue turned away from the table where she was peeling potatoes – to dab at a tear sliding down her face.

"I know, Honey, I know. I lost my mother when I was a little older than you. She died of TB at much too early an age. I was expecting Emma. You know Emma is named for her grandmother. We had lost Barton and then mother and of course, not long after that my husband, Bill, was killed. I've seen a lot of death, and frankly, I don't want to see anymore for a while."

With that little remembrance of sadness, Margie turned to Carol Sue and gave her a robust little squeeze as she put her hands on Carol Sue's shoulders and privately gave God thanks for her lovely daughter-in-law . . . mother-to-be.

~ ~ ~

Things were getting busier by the day at the store. Jason had excellent help with Trey and Jeremy. Clay had come on board too. He really had found a niche in store keeping. They were all pleased and surprised at the difference in Clay's demeanor as a merchant. Trey had become the assistant general manager, next to Jason, and Jeremy pretty much took care of shipments both incoming and outgoing. Clay had surprised them all with his customer care. Clay had always been so quiet and withdrawn. Margie and Jason talked often about Clay's reticence and wondered what they could do to draw him out and help him to relate to people.

Jason loved telling the story of Clay's encounter with the town gossip, Mrs. Dawson. She was a wealthy widow and a "tale carrier." She had just entered the store on her regular Saturday morning "run." Most of the clerks would look the other way and manage to get real busy when they saw her coming. This particular Saturday morning, Clay was on duty. He had just begun his trial as a clerk in the front of the store. When he saw Mrs. Dawson, not realizing how difficult she could be, he rushed up to speak to her and offer his assistance.

"Good morning, Ma'am," Clay cheerfully greeted her.

"I don't know what's good about it, young man, if you consider how cold it's been lately. This kind of weather makes we older citizens ache with the "misery" of arthritis in our bones."

Trying to be nice and helpful, Clay jumped in "where angels fear to tread."

"Why, I wouldn't consider you to be an older citizen, Mrs. Dawson. You don't look a day over fifty."

"Fifty!" Mrs. Dawson chirped. "Young man, I'll have you know I am not a day over fifty. In fact I'm not even close to being fifty."

Clay backed up and coughed as he tried to recover with something good to say and save the day, "I'm sorry, Ma'am. I meant you don't look a day over forty." With that the backing up and shuffling that Clay was doing caught up with him as he backed into the apple barrel, caught his foot in the fringe of a rag rug and fell against the barrel. The whole display came tumbling down and knocked it all over. Apples rolled everywhere and Mrs. Dawson – just threw up her hands and departed. Poor Clay lay there in the middle of the apples, trying hard not to cry, looking around to see if anyone else saw what had just taken place.

Jason happened upon the scene and helped him up as he tried desperately to hold his laughter. "Sorry, Clay, looks like you kinda have a little case of apple-basket-turnover here. And, what happened to your customer."

"She isn't my customer, Jason. I hope I don't have to wait on her again. And, as for the *apple basket turnover,* I'm really not amused."

Clay and Zoe were finishing up their last year of school that spring. Clay had found that being at the store every spare minute was his greatest joy, except for Mrs. Dawson and the apple barrel. He seemed to enjoy talking to the customers, knew where everything was kept and just generally made himself useful. He was turning into a natural-born salesman. Who would have thought?

Zoe was looking forward to continuing her education formally. She had shown a great deal of promise in music and art. She seemed to have her mother's gregarious bent toward music and creativity. Margie had never had time to develop her talents, but she well remembered how much she enjoyed her young years of piano lessons with her cousin, Rosemary. That was over twenty-five years ago. She could still play a little, but Zoe had passed her up and was becoming quite a pianist. Zoe had a wonderful soprano voice and the church choir was quite dependent on her singing and leading the group.

Margie had found a wonderful opportunity for Zoe to study with an older woman who took only five students a year. She believed in a concentrated program of piano and voice and had established a boarding school not too far from Tampico in the neighboring town of Seymour.

Zoe would be enrolled there and begin studies in the fall. It was an exciting time. Not to mention the excitement of love and promise. She and Joshua had secretly pledged themselves to a lifetime together. She was too young to become engaged, but Josh wasn't about to lose "his love," to life and growing up that Zoe still had to negotiate. They had talked of their plans over the Christmas holidays. Josh had given her a sweetheart ring that she wore on a long chain around her neck. Abby had noticed it . . . the romantic that she was at the tender age of twelve. She had asked Zoe about it and Zoe was able to make up a story. Zoe thought she had convinced Abby about how a friend of hers at school and she had traded rings, pledging to be friends forever. Abby wasn't fooled, but she kept Zoe's secret . . . just because. That's what sisters were for . . . keeping each other's secrets.

~ 23 ~

*"Commit you actions to the LORD, and your
plans will succeed."*
Proverbs 16:3

The next few years were filled with family happenings.
Jeremy and Alvina were married the summer after
George and Martin returned from their adventure in the west.
Trey and Carol Sue had welcomed their wonderful baby girl
into the Casey family. All of that had gone very well.

Meanwhile, though life had been filled with other happenings – almost too close for comfort. The huge and horri-
fying fire in Chicago had burned from Sunday, October 8, to
early Tuesday, October 10, 1871. It killed hundreds of people
and destroyed about four square miles of the huge city to the
north. Though the fire was one of the largest U.S. disasters
of the time, the rebuilding began almost immediately. Jason
had been called upon by the governor of Indiana to head up a
committee of merchants and suppliers that could conjure up
the goods and services that were so important to Chicago's
recovery.

It had been good for business and certainly was a compliment to Jason. That is to be recognized by the state's
leaders as one of the most enterprising and capable men of

the area. Jason was gone a great deal. He had stories to tell as he scoured the country working with the state commission to locate and transport building materials two hundred miles north. He didn't talk a lot about the misery and destruction he observed in the aftermath of the disaster. But, Margie knew he was troubled. She tried hard to take up the slack at home and as usual she was a godsend to the family.

~ 24 ~

*"Fear the LORD and serve him wholeheartedly
... Serve the LORD alone. But if you refuse to
serve the LORD, then choose today whom you
will serve ... But as for me and my family,
we will serve the LORD."*
Joshua 24:14-15

~ Spring of 1873 ~

The wedding would be huge! Margie, Renee, Carol Sue, Alvina, Emma and Abby would see to that. When you have six grown women in your family you would not dare to think anything else.

"Oh, Joshua, I am so happy," Zoe was gushing the evening that she got home from the big shopping trip she and her mother had made to Indianapolis. "My dress is thee most gorgeous creation you have ever seen. Not that you've seen many wedding dresses. Have you, Joshua?"

"No, Zoe, I haven't. Most of my friends who married in the past five years didn't have such elaborate weddings. I really don't know why we are," Joshua was not gruff, but he certainly was being a man. "I don't know why we just didn't have Rev. Robertson marry us with the family there and we would already be on our honeymoon."

"Oh, you men, that's all you think about. Honeymoon, honeymoon – and what else - leaving home, moving to that dreadful little house at your church appointment. I mean, I'm happy you have been called to Mount Pisgah, but really, Joshua, I can't imagine how we're going to manage in such small quarters."

Zoe was really letting her spoiled-self show. She had tried to be satisfied with what Joshua had gotten them in to. She had hoped for a bigger church and a bigger place to live, but as Joshua explained, you have to go where you are sent and Mount Pisgah Methodist Episcopal Church was his assignment.

The people there had been kind and were somewhat apologetic that they didn't offer more. Most of them had much better accommodations that what they were willing to provide for their pastor's living quarters. In the midst of all of that, Joshua was considerate and appreciative and, he made up for Zoe's lack of "servant's spirit." Hopefully, this wasn't a bad sign of things to come. Zoe had always had her way and though she had come a long way over the last six years – she was still Zoe - lively, lovely to look at, talented beyond imagination and spoiled.

~ ~ ~

Margie had Clay carry in the packages from the buggy. Clay had met them at the train and they were loaded down with everything imaginable, favors and decorations for the reception, ribbons, special candles and candle holders – the list was inexhaustible. They had found everything on their lists and more.

"Mother, where do you want me to put all this stuff?" Clayton groaned.

"Dining room table, Clay, or on the floor, just get it in the house," Margie called over her shoulder as she carefully carried the huge box that held the wedding gown. She realized it had cost way too much, but after all, Zoe was the first of the girls to marry and she wanted her to have what she wanted. *Was that a mistake? I guess I have always given in to Zoe. Hummmm, hope I haven't gone too far. Oh, no, she'll be fine. Still happiness isn't dependent upon how much something costs.* Margie continued to argue with herself as she just enjoyed the moment and the thrill of the biggest wedding that the county had ever seen.

Jason came in the back door about the time Margie found a place to safely deposit the box with the dress of the century. "Margie, what have you done? Looks like you have bought everything that was loose in the city." Jason didn't really care, but he was surprised. *Margie usually didn't go overboard on anything. Guess once in a blue moon would be okay.*

"Oh, Jason, wait until to you see all the wonderful things we have found for the wedding. I am so excited. Really, Jason, have I spent too much? Do you think I've overdone it?"

"Well, Margie, I . . . uhhhh don't know. Haven't seen any *change* though from the little *fortune* you took with you to shop." He grinned as he walked on through the dining room and up the stairs. He just wanted to put on his work clothes and get out to the stables. One of his prize mares was about to drop her foal. He knew this one would be the prize. In all of his experiences in breeding the American Saddle Horses, this was his prize mare and her sire was the best of the bunch. In three years he would surely have the Indiana State Grand Prize in the American Saddle Horse competition.

Emma and Abby were trying to help Tammy get supper on the table, but the table was covered with packages. "Mother, where do we eat? You've loaded the table with boxes and sacks." Emma was not upset with her mother, but it was a good question.

"Oh, Honey," Margie quickly rushed to help her. "Let's eat in the kitchen tonight. I'm too tired to do another thing. There are just a few of us tonight. Your father won't even be in to eat until he finishes out in the stables. We can fit around the kitchen table."

With that little adjustment, Emma was back in the kitchen arranging plates and silverware on the kitchen table. *Mother has certainly gone overboard with this wedding. I hope Zoe appreciates it. She should – the sky's the limit where she's concerned.* Emma's thoughts were marching back in forth in her generous, but concerned mind.

Emma was the steady one. She was always there to fill in the gaps, carry the cross and bind the wounds. *Well, she did do a lot of mature and unselfish things for everyone else. When would her time come?*

Emma had finished her teacher's training almost two years ago and had already taught one full term and was near the completion of her second year of teaching. She was a natural. The Head Master of the private school in which she taught in Indianapolis, Dr. Byron Harrall, couldn't find anything to criticize about Emma. She was kind, but firm; helpful but challenging. In fact, he secretly wished he wasn't 20 years her senior. His wife had died in child birth over ten years ago and he had been able to take care of his son and daughter, who were now thirteen and ten mostly because his mother had moved in to help him. Mrs. Harrall had been a widow for several years when Byron's Betsy had died. It was all doable for everyone, except the fact that Byron was so lonely. He had filled most of his lonely days and nights with work and really hadn't met anyone that could come close to his Betsy's charm and disposition. That is until he met Emma Wilson. She was a remarkable young woman.

~ ~ ~

Emma was busy dishing up the food and not paying much attention to her mother or Zoe. They were still in their shopping mode and were certainly caught up in their excitement of planning and buying everything in sight. Abby was nosing through some of the packages on the dining room table – when Zoe flounced through the room and reprimanded her pretty severely. Emma heard the racket and called them to supper, hoping that all would settle down soon and they could all regain their good sense.

"So, Zoe, did you leave anything for any other bride to buy in Indianapolis?" Jason had just come downstairs on his way out to the stables. Zoe blushed and thoroughly enjoyed the attention and teasing. She always had. She always would.

"Well, Father," Zoe cooed, "I'm sure we didn't buy it all, but we tried. Didn't we, Mother?"

"Oh, Jason, we didn't purchase anything that wasn't needed. In fact, we left quite a lot in the shops for other brides, and the next time we'll be shopping for Emma . . . right, Dear?" Margie had unintentionally brought it up again. *When was Emma going to have a serious beau?*

Emma felt the scarlet tinge creeping up her throat, as it always did, when she realized she was the center of everyone's attention and they were all waiting for an answer to the question.

"Mother, we've had this conversation before. I'm fine. I love my career. My students are my family and marrying just anyone that comes along is not my idea of happiness. Come on, everyone let's eat. Supper is getting cold."

There, she had avoided this conversation one more time. *Why, why, why do people think they have to interfere with everyone else's lives? I don't do that to people – why do they think they can just nose into a person's business?*

Zoe wasn't letting it go. "Well, I happen to know that Dr. Harrall has a yen to be more friendly with Emma."

"Zoe! Stop it!" Emma whirled around as she set the last bowl on the table. "You don't know any such thing. How could you even think such a thing - much less say it?"

"Okay, girls, that's enough." Margie realized that what she thought was gentle kidding, was causing a row, and that's the last thing she wanted to do.

The rest of the mealtime conversation turned to Abby's day at school and Bart's latest discovery of a very interesting beetle he had managed to capture that afternoon.

Joshua had quietly slipped out for a quick walk before supper. He needed some time to think and try to make sense of all that was happening with Zoe and "the wedding." He had really tried to just stay out of it, but it was really nagging at him. All that money spent on such trivial things when people all over the world were starving. He had thought often of the missionaries that had come and gone throughout his years of schooling. He had even considered becoming a foreign missionary. He was torn between his love for his family, especially his love for Zoe, and the harsh reality of years of separation, possibly never marrying. He had determined that he could serve God right here, near his family, and he could still be with his beloved. The only problem right now, was that *his beloved had turned into a spoiled kettle of catfish.* What to do? *How am I supposed to deal with this overwhelming binge of "stuff, things, and fall-de-rall!" Guess I'd better get back for supper, I'll have to deal with Margie too. She doesn't appreciate tardiness.*

Supper had gone by without anymore drama and Joshua had decided that he would talk to his father after the meal. Maybe his father could shed some light on this *female dilemma.*

Joshua made his excuses to Zoe and caught up with his father. "Dad, I need to talk to you."

"Sure, Joshua, what's going on? Where have you been all afternoon? I didn't see you in the kitchen at suppertime. Do you just have the getting-married-jitters?" Jason was rather enjoying Joshua's expected pre-marriage nerves. After all, wasn't that part of the scenario? Generations of grooms had gone through the same thing. Jason had to endure it twice.

"Well, actually, I'm not concerned about getting married so much as I'm worried about how to think or act toward Zoe and her elaborate preparations. I've tried several times to make sense out of spending so much and well, really going overboard on the finery and the frills."

"I know, son. I saw what the women carried in from their shopping trip. I've been taking it all in these last few weeks. It seems like a snowball rolling downhill, but it will soon be over and life can get back to normal. That's just one of the little trials to be borne with females. Of course women don't have any trials to bear with us men." Jason chuckled as he glanced over his shoulder just in time to see Joshua scratching his head as he mumbled something under his breath.

"Well, I'm telling you, Dad, one wedding is enough for me. I don't even intend to go through another one."

~ 25 ~

"Because of God's grace to me, I have laid the foundation like an expert builder. Now others are building on it. But whoever is building on this foundation must be very careful. For no one can lay any foundation other than the one we already have - Jesus Christ."
I Corinthians 3:10-11

Joshua had a message to meet with his church board the next afternoon. He had hoped that Zoe might go with him, but she had too many things on her schedule. He went alone. Mount Pisgah was only eight miles from Tampico and Joshua had mixed feelings about being "called" to a congregation so near his home. It meant his folks could come once in awhile to hear him preach, but on the other hand "A prophet is without fame in his own country." He might have been better off to be further away from home and family, after all he was grown up, trained, ordained and a totally on his own to lead a church.

When he arrived at the church, there were three wagons and one buggy tied up under the big tree off to the side of the church. He recognized Mr. Owens' buggy. He had met with him when the Superintendent had given him his first opportunity to visit with the congregational members. Mr. Owens was the chairman of the church board and Joshua had gotten along very well with him.

He tied up his horse at the hitching post and entered the front door just in time to hear one of the men say something about "the preacher's young wife." "Good afternoon, gentlemen. Am I late?" Joshua was rather caught off guard and wasn't sure if the discussion and particularly the comment he had heard was friendly or critical.

"No, no, Pastor Casey," Mr. Owens quickly responded. "You're just in time. We were catching up on some things that we've been talking about doing around the church and the parsonage. Glad you're here. Have a seat up here by me. We're glad you're here."

The other four men were somewhat embarrassed wondering if their conversation had been overheard. They had been talking about Zoe and one of them had made the remark about whether or not their new preacher's wife would be a good example as a preacher's wife for their wives and daughters. They had talked about her having been raised in a wealthy family over in Tampico. Actually, they all knew who the Caseys were. And, of course because they were the largest merchants in the area and Jason Casey was a very influential man in the county and state, perhaps his stepdaughter would be spoiled. Even more than that – hadn't Pastor Casey and his wife-to-be been raised in the same household and really were step-brother and sister.

This was not a new discussion. Margie and Jason had talked long and hard with Joshua and Zoe when it first became apparent that they were in love and could be considering marriage. They all knew that everything was as it should be and because Joshua was eleven years older than Zoe, he had only been at home for six years after she had come to be a part of the family when her mother and his father had married. They were no relation except by the marriage of their parents. "Life can be very complicated," Margie summed up that conversation. "You two could have met under other circumstances and there would be no problem whatsoever."

That was Margie. She always tried her best to make the "best" out of every situation. Little did anyone know that Joshua would actually end up being ordained in the Methodist Episcopal Church and that he would even be appointed to a church so near their home.

Mr. Owens cleared his throat and called the meeting to order. "Pastor Casey, we have called this meeting to discuss . . . uh . . . what we believe might become a difficult situation."

"Excuse me, Sir, what are you talking about? What do you mean *what might become a difficult situation?*"

"Well, the fact that your wife is your sister . . . I mean your step-sister. We have had a number of folks come and talk to the different ones of us about . . . uh . . . that it just doesn't seem proper that you two . . . I mean . . . that you and your wife will be man and wife – I mean sister and brother."

Mr. Owens had become confused trying to express the subject of the meeting. With that bewildering attempt to start the meeting, Mr. Owens just hung his head and gave a big sigh.

Joshua was dumbfounded. He didn't know what to say. He looked down and studied his hands as he rubbed over a knot on his finger that had been the result of an accidental slip of the hammer. "Well, Mr. Owens, you and I talked about this when we met last month. I mean the Superintendent knows the . . . uh . . . situation and he didn't have any problem with it. Reverend Robertson had vouched for our family and our circumstances . . . do I need to explain all of that?"

"No, Pastor Casey, you don't. I didn't have any problem with your appointment, but several of our folks have expressed concern and we have voted to ask the Superintendent to send us another pastor. We hope that you understand. As for myself, I am very disappointed. I believe that you are more than qualified and I'm sure your wife . . . er, uh . . . wife-to-be will be a fine . . . uh . . . pastor's wife. I am truly sorry. I hope you understand."

Joshua was speechless. He had been fired before he had even started. He was not given a chance to succeed. He asked himself . . . *What could God be doing? Or was it God's doing?*

"Mr. Owens, Gentlemen, I won't begin to say that I understand, because I don't, but I can't do anything to change this . . . and . . . I pray that someday I will be able to deal with it."

Joshua was gaining some composure as he paused and was gaining strength and perspective . . . "I am sure that God has a plan for my life - for my wife's and my life - and if it doesn't include you or this church . . . I will, one day, be able to forgive this injustice and hope and pray that Mt. Pisgah will have its just due. I'll show myself out. Good day, Gentlemen"

Joshua knew he was walking, but he really couldn't feel anything. *What had just happened? Is that what the Body of Christ does? Is this God's will? What's happening?*

The blue sky somewhat sobered his thoughts and he managed to mount his horse as he rode off toward Tampico . . . still in a daze . . . wondering what would be next? His life had been so well ordered. Since he had been a teenager discussing God with Pastor Robertson he had always felt secure and affirmed. This was a first. Turned away from service where he had been prepared and called to . . . by people who had conjured up, *in the name of God*, a judgment against him, and Zoe, based on nothing . . . absolutely nothing but their small, peevish imaginations.

What would he tell Zoe? That is the worst part. He felt shame, and he hadn't done anything to be ashamed of.

He rode slowly away from the church. Not feeling, not thinking, Joshua was in a state of shock. They didn't prepare pastors for such things as total rejection, especially based on personal opinions that had nothing to do with one's ability to minister.

~ ~ ~

He took the long way home and took a long time stabling his horse. He truly appreciated his father's *love* of the gentle creatures. He could appreciate what it felt like to honor God and care for his creation – perhaps not care for the people, that was a stumbling block right now.

When he entered the back door, there was a great outburst of giggling coming from the parlor. *What's going on now? Zoe is having the time of her life . . . and I . . . well, I'm just having a time! What to do next? Where do I go from here?* He had forgotten that a few of Zoe's closest friends were giving her a personal shower this afternoon. He couldn't imagine what could be so *personal* about a shower. Really?

He had hardly completed that thought when Zoe came bursting into the kitchen just as Joshua was helping himself to a glass of lemonade. "Oh, Dear, I didn't know you were back. How did the meeting go? I'll bet you were wonderful. We're going to have such a great life together, Joshua . . . Joshua," Zoe had finally looked up and realized that Joshua's appearance was somewhat different. In fact, he looked like he had lost his last friend. "Joshua, Honey, what's the matter with you? You look like you've been run over and left for dead."

"Oh, Zoe, I didn't want to tell you like this. I heard you ladies having such a great time when I just came in and I was secretly hoping to avoid any conversation for a while.'

"Joshua, you're scaring me. What are you talking about? What kind of secrets what conversation are you hoping to avoid? My goodness, what's going on?'

"I'll tell you everything later, Honey. You just go back to your party and I'll be out back in the orchard when you have time to talk."

~ 26 ~

*"Look at those who are honest and good for a
wonderful future awaits those who love peace."*
Psalm 37:37

E mma had enjoyed the week-end at home. She was really
glad to get back to her teaching and her private life.
Family is good – at times – and not so good other times. *It's
amazing to me,* Emma thought, *how could people you love
so much be so cruel? I guess they don't mean to be, but I'm
in no hurry to find a man. In fact, I'm not sure I even want to.*

Emma had thought long and hard about what marriage
was like. She well remembered, even though she was a little
girl, when her daddy was trying to farm, and he became more
and more distant day-by-day. She thought about the nights
she lay very still listening to her mother's quiet crying. She
even offered to sleep with her and tell her a bedtime story
to make her mother feel better. Little did she know that her
father's absence, late night drinking, just avoiding life in
general could not be fixed by a four-year-old. She remembered Aunt Renee's sad life too. Neither her husband nor her
son were very good to her. She had learned this as she had
heard her mother and Aunt Renee talking. Emma had gotten
a very difficult start on life concerning men and their role in

the family. Oh, she liked her step-father, Jason, well enough, but even that had been an arranged marriage to give them a place to live and she felt that they, her mother, Zoe, Clay and herself, were "poor relation."

"Emma, what a serious face you have on today," Maryleen had walked into Emma's classroom twenty minutes after school had been dismissed for the day. "I looked for you outside, thought you would be on your way home. Or would you rather just live here?" Maryleen had a joyful banter going most of the time. She was a rather plump, but smallish young woman with red, curly hair and lots and lots of freckles. She and Emma had been friends the year that they roomed together at the Normal School Teachers' Training Institute. They had both been hired to teach, along with two other teachers, at the American Academy for Higher Learning. It was a new private school that had been founded in conjunction with Claremont College in Indianapolis. It was a boarding school for young women, very expensive and very exclusive. The Head Master was Dr. Byron Harrall, Ph D. He had been on the faculty of Claremont College and was assigned the formidable task of integrating and preparing young women for Claremont College entrance at the end of the four year curriculum upon graduation from the American Academy.

It had only been a little over 30 years that schooling was available to the general public or even affordable in private schools. The publication of the <u>Common School Journal</u>, published by Horace Mann in Massachusetts, had taken the educational issues to the public. While schools in the states along the eastern seaboard had passed the first compulsory school attendance laws around 1852, those laws had not been so well defined and in place in the Midwest.

There were grade schools sprinkled throughout the country sides that managed to offer grades one through six or eight to the local children, opportunities beyond that were almost always only available in private schools. The American Academy was proving to be one of the finest in the Midwest. It was a privilege and an opportunity for someone like Emma to be hired to teach there. She was also attending classes at Claremont. She and her brothers and sisters had been given several years of education beyond the eighth grade in Tampico. A husband and wife from London, England, had settled in Tampico as an experiment in developing and teaching curriculum beyond the grade school levels. It had been a great success and many of the youth from Jackson County had advanced beyond the average education available in the surrounding areas.

Emma loved teaching. She was a natural-born teacher. She was also a lovely young woman who knew her worth and she guarded herself, her thoughts and her actions with a clear resolve. She had determined that path for herself at an early age and so far, she had succeeded. While her mother was a very bright and gifted woman, she had not evolved into the thinking that allowed her to accomplish, or even strive to accomplish, many learned skills or professions outside of the realm of marriage. Being married, rearing children, supporting your family and your community were and are among the most noble contributions that a woman can make, but Emma knew there could be more. She hoped to prove it.

Maryleen piped up again, "Emma, I'll say it again. What has come over you? Ever since your trip home last weekend, you have become so serious and almost morose. Did someone hurt your feelings?"

"Oh, no, Maryleen, my feelings aren't hurt. I guess you could say my sensibilities are though. Why is it that people think that every woman should be married and if they aren't there's something wrong with them?"

"You tell me. I have the same mantra said over me every time I'm around my mother, my aunt and my grandmother. I'm surprised they let me out of the house without a man at my side. I might decide to go completely wild or just waste my whole life doing good." With that last sarcastic comment, Maryleen laughed her inimitable, lovely laugh and Emma smiled wider and wider until she broke into a delightful chuckle as well.

"Let's go shopping, Maryleen, my mother gave me some "walking around money," as she calls it. I think she just felt guilty because she's spending so much on my sister Zoe's wedding. I might just buy me a man. If I could get one to my specifications it would be worth it."

"Mercy, Emma, how much money would that take? I'll start saving today. I might even get an extra job." They both laughed as they linked arms and went out into the world, free as two breezes and ready to challenge all comers.

They had barely turned the corner on Washington Street, when they nearly ran into Dr. Harrall. "Good afternoon, ladies, excuse me, I didn't expect such a whirlwind to come around the corner. Where are you two ladies off to in such a hurry? It must be very important."

"Oh, yes sir, it is, Dr. Harrall. Emma and I are off to shop for men." Maryleen, realized what she had said and before she could recover, Dr. Harrall squinted one eye, shook his head in little jerks and said, "What? What did you say, Miss Keyes? Shop for men?"

"No, no, sir, I said hop to the pen . . . uhhhh . . . you know . . . uh . . . the pen place. It's over a few blocks toward Meridian, a nice little place to buy a pen. We both need new pens, right Emma?"

Maryleen elbowed Emma who was too stunned to even speak much less make any sense.

"Uhhhh, uhhhh, yes, that's right new pens . . . we need them . . . have money to pay, I mean spend, I mean, Good Afternoon, Dr. Harrall. Nice to see you."

They hurried on down the street and Dr. Harrall stood for a few minutes looking after them, almost grinning out loud as he pondered the strange conversation and spoke to his heart with words of *admiration, longing to be young again and just plain joy.* That's what being in Emma Wilson's presence did for him . . . always gave him joy. He knew it was joy because he hadn't had a lot of that for a long time.

Byron Harrall had grown up as the youngest of five children in the country very near Indianapolis. He had seen his father work himself literally to death, farming, striving to feed seven mouths. He had determined as soon as he was able he would leave said "country toil" and become educated in some meaningful profession, preferably the law. If not the law, then teaching. That's what he had done.

The Harralls were fine, upstanding people. They had migrated from Scotland in the 18th century and had claimed the land through generations of farmers and particularly successful in raising of pure-bred livestock. That is some of the family had accomplished that enviable task.

Charles Harrall, Byron's father, had not been so blessed. His life seemed to be one long struggle with the land, the small farm that he had inherited. He gave it his best and his best was not good enough to allow him to survive. He died in his early forties and his wife, left with five children of varying ages managed to raise them all. The older ones helped the younger ones and Byron fared the best. At least he had accomplished his dream and had managed to complete his education which led him to his present position with a doctorate of philosophy in higher learning.

His life and his success had been severely marred, however, with the loss of his dear wife, Betsy, leaving him to rear his two young children.

Byron was rather tall, unlike his two older brothers who had taken after their father at least in their stature. Byron was very healthy and well muscled for a learned man. He had always worked at his physical health, remembering that his father's strength had played out when he was only forty.

Byron had a full head of curly light brown hair and a smile that would stop a train. His eyes were quite mischievous for a serious-minded educator, but it served him well. He had a wonderful personality although he was rather sad at times. Mourning his loss and living in a lonely state, he was somewhat affected by it all.

~ 27 ~

"When you go through deep waters, I will be with you. When you go through rivers of difficulty, you will not drown. When you walk through the fire of oppression, you will not be burned up; the flames will not consume you."
Isaiah 43:2

Joshua was just nearing the house from his "turn" through the orchard when his father pulled up in the lane. His day was finished at the store and the best part of his day was just beginning as he hoped to change his clothes and get to the stables to check on the mare.

Jason didn't get to the back door of the house before Joshua had hailed him as he hurried across the back yard. He had been walking and praying and praying and walking. God was stirring his heart and he knew he needed to seek his father's counsel before he talked to anyone else. He and his dad had always been close even though Joshua had subjected his dad and his whole family, really, to his period of "unbelief." That is to say, he had hung back from the family's approach to faith in God and the practice of a life lived in faith. Pastor Robertson had been a tremendous help to him. He had taken Joshua under his wing and patiently, with tremendous insight, guided him to the edge of a redeeming faith. The Holy Spirit had done the rest. That's the way it works. No human being can "save" or convince another human being of how to embrace faith in God, but we certainly can be present in the course that leads to "the place." God does the rest.

It's rather an interesting theological understanding that John Wesley spoke, wrote, preached and believed in what he called *Prevenient Grace*. That is the Grace of God that goes before an individual is even aware of the grace of God. It's a presiding, pursuing action of God, through the Holy Spirit, that *woos us to embrace God as Creator, Savior and Sustainer of our lives here and now – until the "there and then."*

Jason had found that place and his faith was strong. He had answered a call on his life to preach, nurture, care for God's flock – and now – the flock had turned on him.

"Dad, wait up! I need to talk to you."

Jason paused. He always had time for his children. His Heavenly Father had always had time for him – and he could do no less. "What's going on, Joshua, you look like you've been out there working in the orchard, lots of weeds or worse yet, thorns and briars?"

"Well, really the human kind of thorns and briars and probably a few weeds as well. The brethren or as you would say the *cisterns* of Mount Pisgah have been pontificating. They called a board meeting, invited me today so they could fire me."

"Joshua, what are you talking about? The Superintendent has appointed you to serve that church – what in the world do you mean?'

"It seems that *several of the people have been talking* and the short of the long of it – is that they object to my marriage to Zoe. They consider it to be improper. She is my sister, and we grew up in the same family, etc. etc. etc. Brother Owens was very nice, obviously it wasn't his doing. He was kind enough to me – but the others couldn't look me in the eye."

"Joshua, what did you say?" Jason was dumb-founded. He couldn't imagine in a thousand years what had prompted all of this. They had talked about this. They had prayed as a family. They had counseled with Pastor Robertson, and everyone agreed it was proper, acceptable, wonderful and otherwise not a problem.

"I don't even remember what I said, Father. I was so shocked. I don't think I was outwardly angry, but I certainly was seething inside. I said something about *not under-standing, that the Superintendent knew all about our lives,* and oh, I said, *that it was an injustice and that I hoped I would be able to forgive them someday.* Then I just excused myself and, honestly, Father, I don't know how I got out of there. It must have been God that carried me. I rode for a long time. When I got home, Zoe found me in the kitchen and she knew something was wrong, but she, they . . . were in the middle of a giggling bout and I put her off 'til later."

"Well, that was the right thing to do . . . I mean about Zoe. We need to talk this through and make a plan that will cause the least amount of concern or embarrassment for anyone, including the Mount Pisgah people. . . Mercy! I would never have believed this."

"You wouldn't?! I can't believe it yet. It's so . . . so . . . mean spirited. It's so unnecessary. Why, Father, why would people think such things? They're accusing us of horrible things. They're calling us sinners and untoward people. They're . . ." as Joshua paused for a breath . . . Jason took back the conversation.

"Josh, don't go off the deep end. We need to think through this and even more importantly we need to pray through this. Let's you and I go see Pastor Robertson before we talk to anybody."

"Let me stick my head in the door and tell Margie that we're leaving. We'll take the buggy. It's still hitched up." With those instructions, Jason, walked toward the house and Joshua headed for the buggy.

Pastor Robertson was home and was glad to see the men . . . thinking . . . *How unusual to see the Caseys in the late afternoon on a Saturday . . . hummm . . .* "Good afternoon, gentlemen, what brings you both out this fine evening?"

"Pastor, Joshua has had quite a shock this afternoon. We're seeking some wise counsel and probably some much needed comfort." Jason spoke boldly as they were ushered through the front door of the parsonage.

"What's happened, Joshua, everybody all right at home?"

"Oh, yes sir . . . yes . . . we're all fine just, well, as Father said, I'm in shock. I guess you could say. I was called to a meeting at Mount Pisgah this afternoon and the board members met me there to tell me they had . . . well, it's hard for me to even say it . . . they had voted to ask the Superintendent to send them another pastor."

"Joshua, what in the world, prompted that? They couldn't have objected to your preaching . . . yet . . . excuse me . . . I guess that's not really funny. But, I cannot imagine. What was that all about?"

"Pastor Robertson, they claimed that a number of people had come to them and registered concern that Zoe and I were not a fit couple to be in the parsonage so to speak. While they claimed they understood that while we are not really related, we are considered brother and sister, and they didn't feel that was acceptable. Mr. Owens did the talking and he said he had no objections himself, but the consensus was that the congregation would not accept us."

"Joshua, I am shocked too. I guess that makes two of us that have been given a deadly blow this afternoon. I cannot imagine what they think is real and not real. Well, on the other hand, as long as I've been in the ministry . . . I guess

I shouldn't be surprised at anything that people, who by the way call themselves Christians, will do. I am so sorry, Son, I cannot begin to tell you. My Lord and my God, have mercy . . . have mercy . . ." Pastor Robertson's voice trailed off as he knit his brow and rubbed his hands together. He got up from the chair in which he had been sitting and walked the floor. As he paced you could see his mind working.

"Let's get in touch with the Superintendent. Really I can't believe that he hasn't been in touch with you. Did they say they had talked to him?"

"Yes, they indicated that they had already asked him to replace me. Sir, I don't think I could go there and take Zoe and be subjected to such ridicule and misunderstanding."

"No, Joshua, I don't mean . . . no . . . never would expect you to try to serve such pig-headed people. We should rename the church Pigshead instead of Pisgah, as in swine. Casting his eyes upward, *Excuse me, Lord, I'm sorry I've called your flock pig-heads.* I was just thinking that the best action is always to keep the lines of communication open. He should know, if he doesn't, what one of his flocks is up to. He's in charge . . . we're not! That's a blessing!"

Joshua was beginning to feel better already. *If a man of God like John Robertson could express such concern and shock . . . and question such unbelievable actions . . . well, it just makes you feel better.*

"What's your counsel, Jason? This is your family . . . I can't believe this . . ." walking a little faster back and forth and putting his feet down a little harder as he walked . . . he appeared to be a man half-possessed.

"My counsel, well, I haven't had a whole lot of time to think about it, but I really feel personally attacked. I mean Margie and I have raised these children with good Christ-like morals. They have all been faithful to the church and to us . . . I just don't know what to think. And, talking about

Margie, I don't know how she's going to take this. It really is an affront to and on us all."

"Yes, yes! I agree!" Pastor Robertson stopped pacing long enough to look at Jason and give a vigorous, affirmative nod. "Let's pray on it, sleep on it and try to avoid as much confusion and anger as possible. In fact, do you think we can wait until after church tomorrow to make a call on the Superintendent. I'll send a message to him this evening telling him to expect us tomorrow in the early afternoon."

"Oh, thank you, sir," Joshua the first to speak. "I really appreciate your kind concern. I do feel better. I'll just tell Zoe that it will hold until tomorrow. Maybe she can enjoy the rest of the day and evening and bask in the *presence of* her presents. That girl does love presents." With that little bit of mirth, they all had a quiet laugh and the relief began to flow - THEY HAD A PLAN!

"Let's pray, gentlemen." Joshua and his Father both stood with heads bowed and hats in hand. "Father, you know our needs before we ask and our ignorance in asking. . . " Pastor Robertson began . . . "and as we stand here before you in utter amazement at the behavior of your flock, we ask for peace in our hearts, strength in our souls and rest in our minds as we wait upon you. We pray this prayer in the strong and wonderful name of Jesus Christ, Our Lord. Amen"

"Amen!" Jason and Joshua intoned.

"Tomorrow, then after church, Pastor, Joshua and I will come by. We should go together," Jason concluded the meeting and Joshua reached out to take Pastor Robertson's hand as both of his hands encased Pastor Robertson's hand as though if he, Joshua, held on well enough he could take this godly man with him and he would survive.

~ 28 ~

*"Don't be concerned about the outward beauty of
fancy hairstyles, expensive jewelry, or beautiful
clothes. You should clothe yourselves instead with
the beauty that comes from within, the unfading
beauty of a gentle and quiet spirit, which is so
precious to God."*
I Peter 3:3-4

E mma and Maryleen had finished up their mini-shopping
spree with a chocolate soda at the corner drug store.
They had really had a "teenage" experience laughing and
recounting their near miss with Dr. Harrall. He was a dear
man, but he always seemed too serious.

"That's the way you would have to act if you had "Doctor"
before your name, Emma. It just makes more sense. I mean
after one works that hard and that long and writes a thesis,
for heaven's sake . . . he did write a thesis, didn't he? Well,
I mean, you can't just go around cracking jokes all the time.
You must be . . . ahhhh . . . with her nose in the air *DIGG-
NAHH-FIEDD!*"

That sent them both off on another round of giggles as
they sucked the very last chocolaty juices from the bottom of
their tall, cold glasses.

"Maryleen, you must stop this . . . I've laughed so hard, my sides hurt." Emma was absolutely enjoying every minute of it. It has been way too long since she had just thrown all caution to the wind and laughed with a friend. "I can't wait to wear my new shirt waist to class tomorrow. I love azure blue. It reminds me so much of the sky, which reminds me of God, which reminds me that I have to finish my study of Philippians. I'm expected to present tomorrow at assembly. How did I get corrupted so quickly? Must be the devil tempting me."

"No, Emma, the devil camps with me – you're a saint – but even saints like new shirt waists, chocolate sodas and uppity head masters." That set them off again.

Emma reasoned she would be lucky if she could stand up and walk. She felt drunk with relief and happiness.

The girls toddled on back to their tiny apartments. You really couldn't call them apartments, but they did have privacy and freedom in their own spaces. They ate most of their meals in the dining rooms with the students. It was a pleasant life, somewhat demanding, but if being single and free from all responsibility except your career, it was doable.

Emma was surprised to find an ivory colored envelope neatly fastened to her door knob with a brightly colored ribbon. She couldn't miss it. Maryleen didn't see it, her quarters were closer to the stairs coming up to the second floor. Emma's room was further down the hall.

She speculated as she carefully untied the ribbon to free the envelope - *My goodness, who in the world could be leaving her such a mysterious but delightful missile?* She carefully, loosened the sealed flap and extracted the neatly, folded note from the envelope. *Hummmm . . . one of her students . . . a secret admirer . . . not the family . . . they were far too busy with the Zoë Affair. . .* "My heavenly days!" She gasped aloud as she stole a glance at the signor – she clamped her hand over her mouth - although, there was no one present to hear her. "I can't believe this!" She quickly looked up and down the hallway to see if anyone was close by – as she scooted on inside her room.

Dear Emma, (the note began)

I am taking great liberties in penning this note, I sincerely hope you understand, my intentions are honorable and above board. I don't feel speaking to you in public would be appropriate, and there isn't any place in the near vicinity that isn't public to someone from the Academy. So I take my disappearing courage and my tender heart to task and have written this note to just say how much I admire you. It has been a long, long time since I have had any thought(s) whatsoever of discovering someone of the opposite gender. You have made a large impact on my sensibilities (There's that word I reckoned with last week at home – *sensibilities.*) . . . (continuing) *You have made a large impact on my sensibilities and I have taken the privilege, hopefully that is proper, to say these things to you. I realize that I am much older than you . . . and that you are barely older in numeric years than my son, but I feel you are indeed an "old soul." I hope you aren't offended by that . . . the old soul reference. It's a compliment. I have been an educator for the past twenty years and I have rarely found men or women with your honesty and integrity and of course your wit and your charm. Please, again, I pause to ask your forgiveness for such a brazen overture as this. I'll close by saying if you have any interest at all in coming to know me better as a man or even just a friend, I will count myself among the most fortunate. If you prefer to maintain only a professional relationship – I will honor that with all my heart. Thank you for reading and I pray understanding what I am trying to convey. Yours sincerely, friend or more? Byron Harrall*

Emma had held her breath throughout the entire reading of "thee note." She was barely breathing now. *How could I have been so blind? Even Zoe knew Dr. Harrall - Byron,* seemed to be interested in me as a woman. *She only met him on a visit to the Academy and a reception we all attended afterwards. Where have I been? Speaking of sensibilities – mine certainly was unaware of this possibility.*

She sat on the bed for a long time with the note neatly folded and placed back in the envelope. She opened it and read it again. It still said the same thing. *What am I supposed to do now? How do I get up tomorrow and go about my duties? What if I run into Dr. Harrall . . . uhhhh . . . Byron? How shall I act?*

Emma finally recovered and got up and poured some water in her basin and patted her face with the cool, wet cloth. *My goodness, look at my face. It's blood red. I must be embarrassed. But, how could that be? Nobody knows I've received a note . . . a love note . . . from my Supervisor – Head Master – Man About the World – What am I to do? To think?*

Oh, please, God I wish my mother was here. Oh, but You are here, Lord. You never forsake me. You know everyone's heart. You must have known about this all along. (Emma laughed gently) *But, of course you knew about it. You know everything about us. What is that my favorite Psalm says? "You have known me since before I was being knit together in my mother's womb, you know everything about me . . . my standing up . . . my lying down . . .my coming in. . . going out . . . how marvelous are you works, O Lord."*

It was as though Emma knew God's presence. He was there . . . she didn't hear a voice, but she knew that God was speaking to her heart. *Hold on my child, joy comes in the morning.*

Hold on? Joy comes in the morning! *I know that Scripture it comes from the 30th Psalm.*

JOY COMES IN THE MORNING! *Well, I can hardly wait!*

~ 29 ~

*"Once you were full of darkness, but now you
have light from the LORD. So live as people of
light! For this light within you produces only
what is good and right and true."*
Ephesians 5:8-9

J ason and Joshua hardly spoke on the ride home. They did
decide to go calmly about the rest of the evening and not
to say more than that they were working on a problem which
had come up and Pastor Robertson was leading them, in fact
asking, them to be a part of it . . . not to worry.

Zoe rushed out to meet them, "Joshua, where have you
been? You were here for a minute and gone. I've been worried."

"Well, you needn't worry about me, Zoe, I'm perfectly
capable of taking care of myself, been doing it for a long
time." Joshua was a little short with her. He was completely
perturbed, not Zoe's fault, but she was in the *space* where
he needed to *walk through*. That is to say, he didn't need to
be pinned down or penned up either one. He just needed to
survive the next twenty-four hours.

137

Jason came to the rescue, "Where's your mother, Zoe? Have you ladies completed your partying for the day? It seems like you ladies are have too much fun."

It helped to relieve the tension for the moment, but Jason could feel the anger and the hurt emanating from Joshua ten feet away. Zoe could have felt it too, except she was so wrapped up in her own joy and frivolity right now, she couldn't sense anything else.

"Mother is trying to make sense of the kitchen. The party ran over just a bit and refreshments are still all over the place. I think she's trying to get supper started."

"Well, that's good news. I could eat the south end of a northbound bear about now," Jason joked. Joshua looked at his father like *What are you talking about? How can you make jokes at a time like this?*

Jason winked at him and kept walking toward the stables. He needed to unhitch his trusty and faithful friend that did his job so well and make him comfortable before he took care of anything else. He needed to check on the mare too. He'd nearly forgotten about her. She probably would drop her foal tonight. Things always seemed to come in bunches when you were the least expecting them – or need more excitement.

Joshua turned back toward the house and Zoe moved toward him. She had been left out of something and she knew it. It was time for her to find out. Zoe plied her feminine wares on Joshua as she snuggled up to him. Joshua managed to smile at Zoe and put his arm around her as they flirted. He felt better just being close to her. "So, you sat around all afternoon and sipped punch, ate cookies and opened more and more and more presents, Miss Zoe? What are you going to do for entertainment when the wedding AMEN has been spoken and we're old married folks?"

"Oh, Josh, you know you love it. I know you love me . . . you do don't you?" Zoe skipped around in front of Joshua and batted her long luscious eye lashes as only she could. She was a temptress. She knew what her talents were and she used them. Joshua loved that about her. She excited him and made him feel like he was her protector as well as her friend and to be lover.

"Well, hello there," Margie stepped off the back porch onto the sidewalk. "Where's your father?" I hardly knew he had come home, and then he was gone again. What's so important that you two rushed off?"

"Oh, we . . . well, really I, had some business with Pastor Robertson and Dad went with me. We have to finish it up tomorrow after church. It's just men stuff to do with the church."

"Hummmm, sounds a bit ominous to me," Margie commented. "But, then I never have understood exactly what *men stuff* is. Guess I'm too old to start worrying about that now."

With that little tidbit, she made her way back through the porch and into the kitchen. Zoe was right, the kitchen was a shambles and a meal had to be set out. The family had always been large with ten mouths to feed, eleven counting Tammy, and with Trey and Jeremy married and Emma gone, it was still eight since Bart had been added to the flock.

Tammy was way ahead of Margie, always faithfully following, picking up, quietly going about her business. What would they have done all these years without her?

Jason came in the back door about that time and surprised Margie with a quick squeeze of the waist and a peck on the back of her neck. "Jason Casey, what in the world are you up too? You sure are frisky!"

"Don't know, Love of My Life, I guess spring is in the air and love is in bloom! These young people aren't the only ones around here." He chuckled as he headed on through the kitchen, bounding up the stairs to wash up and get ready for supper.

The meal was fairly quiet. Margie thought Joshua was unusually quiet, but then she could never read him anyway. Clay was late to the table as usual. She didn't say anything to him. She really was tired of all the years of trying to corral him. Who could do it? She hadn't succeeded. Characteristics do run in families. He reminded her so much of his father. Bill Wilson had been a strange one. She thought it was just his upbringing. What a hard life he had lived, but watching Clay all these years, she realized it was a family trait. Clay could never be understood . . . moody, pensive and withdrawn much of the time.

After supper, Margie shooed everybody out of the dining room so she could have some peace. She'd rather help Tammy clean up than listen to all the banter and polite arguing that usually followed supper. She really did wonder though where the men had gone this afternoon and why they seemed to be so different in their demeanor. Jason would tell her later. She'd just have to wait.

~ 30 ~

*"This hope will not lead to disappointment.
For we know how dearly God loves us, because
he has given us the Holy Spirit to fill our
hearts with his love."*
Romans 5:5

E mma had survived the night, but just barely. She tossed
and turned and dreamed and imagined in between
dreams. *What was the strange feeling that had come over
her? It couldn't be love, but it certainly was exciting. What
was it that Byron, uhhhh Dr. Harrall has said? He admires
me. He wants to be more than friends. He thinks I'm what?
. . . Joy comes in the morning. Well, we'll see. Right now, I
need to get myself out of this bed and get ready for the day –
whatever it may bring.*

Emma hadn't finish dressing when she heard a familiar
rap on the door, "You-hoo, Emma, it is I, Maryleen. May I
come in?"

"Sure, Maryleen, enter at your own risk." Emma was
feeling quite frisky.

"What's on your agenda for today, Emma? I mean
besides your classes. I really need to have some time to talk

to you. Something really bizarre has occurred and I need a friend's shoulder to lean on."

Emma wondered what in the world Maryleen could have happening in her life that was *bizarre. If she only knew about Dr. Harrall's note, love letter . . . no . . . note.*

"Well, I'm finished at 3:30, we can go for a cup of tea then," Emma was trying to keep her voice calm, well-modulated, safe, not giving any clues to her excited spirit.

"Great! I'll meet you in the lobby downstairs at 3:30 or close by."

Emma finally finished dressing, taking extra pains to choose something that befit the occasion, whatever the occasion might be. Who knows? Yesterday certainly didn't start out knowing that it would end with a colossal burst of something or other. Emma really couldn't think straight. *How will she act when she encounters Byron? Well, it remains to be seen.*

Breakfast was uneventful. Regular fare, porridge, muffins, bacon (if you so chose) and coffee. She was surprised that she was so hungry and that it all tasted so good. It was an amazing day. Her heart was singing . . .

There's a bright golden haze on the meadow, there's a bright golden haze on the meadow, the corn is as high as an elephant's eye, and it looks like it's climbing what up to the sky. Oh, what a beautiful morning. Oh, what a beautiful day. I have a wonderful feeling, everything's going my way. Where did that come from? Is this how a heart sings?

Her classes went well all day. Lunch was normal, soup, fresh bread, fruit and milk. And, then, she saw him. He was standing in the entrance of the dining room. There was really nothing unusual about that. He always seemed to give the dining room a quick scan as he stood framed in the doorway. She didn't want to be caught looking at him. Oh, he was coming her direction. *What to do? Oh, mercy . . . what am I going to say?*

"Good afternoon, Emma," Dr. Harrall walked up to her table.

"Oh, hello, Dr. Harrall, how nice to see you here . . . uhhhh . . . well, of course, I would expect to see you here, I mean, every day we are both here . . . uhhhh . . . ."

"Emma, it's nice to see you too. I just stopped by to ask you if you would have dinner with me this evening. I thought we could go to the little café over by Central Park. We can walk and I've heard they have excellent fare."

"Oh, yes, that would be nice . . . what time . . . ? I mean supper time is what time?" Emma continued to effuse as her throat reddened with embarrassment.

"Six would be good, Emma. I'll meet you in the lobby of the residence hall. Or you would prefer to meet me some place else?"

"Well, let's see. How about meeting outside the front at six?" Emma was thinking how it would look to others if she was meeting, greeting and leaving with Dr. Harrall from the lobby.

"Six it is – outside . . . looking forward to it." And, Dr. Harrall was off in a dash . . . very dashing himself.

~ *31* ~

"Be careful to live properly among your unbelieving neighbors. Then even if they accuse you of doing wrong, they will see your honorable behavior, and they will give honor to God when he judges the world."
I Peter 2:12

C hurch as usual . . . everyone talking, laughing enjoying a beautiful spring day. Jason and Joshua were unusually quiet, and Margie knew something was up. She had been around men all of her life and was able to realize that it didn't take much to alter their normal behavior. They were not nearly as adept as women in covering up their feelings or their worries.

Joshua and his father had talked a little about the afternoon's plan while they were hitching the horses to the carriage. "I don't know, Father, I really don't expect anything to change, I guess I just hope to have a say."

"Well, that's important, Son. You really have to seek justice when an injustice has been done. I wouldn't want to think I had raised a son that wouldn't step up and have his say. You know, Joshua, you can say anything that needs to be said if you say it in love. I'm proud of you and Zoe and we will stand together and God will direct us."

"Thanks, Dad, I feel better this morning. Zoe hasn't really caught on to my malaise. She's so enjoying the excitement of the wedding and parties. I guess that's due her. Every girl should be able to enjoy this time in her life. I'm just glad that you and Pastor Robertson are willing to stand with me and I'm looking forward to putting this behind and moving on."

Margie came herding the brood out the backdoor. "We're going to be late and there's no excuse for that." Abby and Barton were following close behind and Zoe and Clay were bringing up the rear. "Come on, children, put a little life in your step . . . church won't wait on us."

With all of that carrying on – they got on their way and were soon settled in the pew with neighbors and friends enjoying their time of worship together. Pastor Robertson waxed eloquently that morning with the Old Testament reading coming from Proverbs 3:5-6 about . . . *"Trusting in the Lord with all your heart and leaning not unto your own understanding, but in all your ways acknowledge God and he will direct your paths."* The Gospel message was taken from Jesus' sermon in Matthew regarding "casting your pearl before swine." Joshua realized that what he and Zoe had was valuable and wonderful and was not to be thrown down or taken lightly. Certainly he was not to allow people who were *small of mind* and *absent of understanding and grace* to get the better of them. God had called them to service and God would see that done.

Sunday dinner was fairly quiet, and Jason and Joshua were unusually quiet, anxious to get on with their chore. Zoe was anxious to work on the wedding favors and décor. Abby would help and between Margie, Carols Sue, Alvina and Renee they would be well done and well ready in plenty of time.

Jason and Joshua went by Pastor Robertson's so he could ride with them and it took them a little over an hour to get to Crothersville where Superintendent Owens lived. They pulled up in front of his house and he came out on the porch to meet them. "Oh, gentlemen, come in, come in. Good to see you."

Well, what did that mean? All three of the visitors, men with a mission, wondered in their own individual ways what the warm welcome could possibly mean. Or did Superintendent Owens just now realize what had taken place?

As they settled themselves in the Owens' living room, Mrs. Owens made herself scarce and wasn't to be seen or heard from again. Reverend Owens cleared his throat and began with, "Now, exactly what brings you gentlemen over for this visit today?"

Pastor Robertson spoke up first, "Reverend Owens, I think you are aware of the decision of Mount Pisgah. They called Joshua into a meeting of the leadership last Saturday afternoon to tell him that they had asked you to send them another pastor."

"Oh, uhhhh, well, yes, that is true that they asked me to send them another pastor, but I haven't appointed anybody else. I just assumed that they would work that out."

"Excuse me, but let me make sure I understand what you're saying. You assumed that when these congregational leaders directly told you to appoint another pastor that they wouldn't accept Joshua and his wife, Zoe, that you would not do what they asked and that you just assumed that they would change their minds and treat Joshua and Zoe with grace? Is that what you're telling us?"

"Well, I guess . . . yes . . . that's about it." Reverend Superintendent Owens seemed to be squirming just a bit.

Joshua hadn't said a word and Jason was biting his lip to keep his mouth shut.

Pastor Robertson continued, "Well, Sir, that is not acceptable. It's not Christian and, it's not going to resolve this matter."

Pastor Robertson had been a District Superintendent. He had been a good one too. He was less than a year from retiring and frankly he didn't have much patience with the likes of Reverend Owens.

"I, uhhhh, I see your point." Owens spluttered. "I don't really know what to do about this, John." They were now on a first-name basis. "I know that Reverend Casey is a fine man and I had hoped that this would be good for him and the church."

"Well, it isn't working and they have embarrassed him beyond what is acceptable and as far as I'm concerned they don't even deserve a pastor. The very idea that they thought that Joshua and Zoe, having been raised by two of the finest people in this part of the world, would be anything but upstanding young people, called to the work of the Lord, is beyond me."

"Yes, I see your point." Owens addressing, Joshua, said, "Young man you haven't said anything. How do you feel about this?"

"Reverend Owens, I'm not even sure I can feel. I'm still in shock. I went directly to Pastor Robertson and he asked me to wait until we talked to you today. My father and I have kept all of this to ourselves and haven't even shared it with my step-mother or my fiancé. Our main concern is the church, as it should be, however, I don't feel they have treated me or my wife-to-be with Christian love or concern. Frankly, I don't think I could ever be their pastor knowing how they feel about us. I don't know what's to become of my "call" to ministry. I guess that's up to you."

Nodding his head, Reverend Owens looked over to Reverend Robertson and asked him, "John, what do you suggest?"

"I don't know. I don't think that it would be good for Joshua or Zoe to serve within this district or perhaps even the conference. I think he should probably look further and I intend to help him. We only wanted you to know what the situation is of this date and wish you some measure of wisdom as you, and you alone, try to work it out."

With that pronouncement, Reverend Robertson stood as if he was washing his hands of the whole affair, leaving it with the Superintendent and his non-Christian, non grateful church.

Owens began fussing around, trying to talk to Jason. He knew who Jason was. Jason's reputation preceded him and his affluence even surpassed his reputation. Owens knew that he was the biggest contributor in the whole district. That's why the church in Tampico had done so well, especially in its mission outreach. What a mess!

Jason, Joshua and Pastor Robertson said their good-byes and departed rather quickly leaving Owens standing in the middle of the front porch like a sputtering candle – about to go out.

The ride home was quiet for a while and then as the silence lessened, Jason spoke first, "Well, Pastor Robertson, if I ever had a doubt about your fairness, your wisdom and feel for justice, I certainly wouldn't have one now. I can't thank you for your help and standing forth for Joshua and Zoe and really just putting Reverend Owens in his rightful place."

Joshua made some remarks agreeing and Pastor Robertson stopped him with a very exciting proposition. "Don't worry, Joshua, I have some ideas that I've been mulling around through the night, last night. I believe that you should look further than the local church. While the experience, under normal circumstances, is invaluable, I believe that with your brilliance and willingness to serve the Lord, you should be teaching others. With your permission, I'm going to write the President of Wesleyan Theological Seminary and inquire about a position for you. It will not pay a lot in dollars, but it will be invaluable to the church for you to be there."

"Thank you, sir. I sincerely appreciate your help. I have secretly wished for that to happen one day, but I was perfectly willing to pay my dues in the local church. I know that it's important to be in ministry on a daily basis, involved and helping people with their lives in faith and obedience to God."

"Not to worry, Joshua. It will take some time, but in the meantime, after the wedding and honeymoon why don't you plan on partnering with me while we make the inquiries and work out your future."

At this juncture in the conversation, Jason chimed in with words of appreciation for the entire encounter and the hope for the future.

As they arrived back in Tampico, they took Pastor Robertson home and got home just in time for Margie's call to supper. The ladies had been busy all afternoon and now it was time to stop and enjoy a family meal, looking forward to some rest in the evening. Joshua was very pleased that Zoe was still involved with a joyful heart and they would have time to embrace the changes that had come up so quickly in their plans.

~ 32 ~

*"Choose a good reputation over great riches;
being held in high esteem is better than
silver or gold."*
Proverbs 22:1

Right on time, as would be expected, both Emma and Byron appeared in front of the Student Residence. Emma had taken great pains in choosing her costume for the evening and she had shared with Maryleen just a little about the evening's activity. Maryleen was about to swallow herself and Emma pledged her to the greatest of discretion for the time being.

"I don't want anybody going off half-cocked," Margie told her. "I certainly don't think *anything* about anything, but that Dr. Harrall asked me for supper. He probably wants to talk about some change in curriculum."

"Oh, sure! I'm absolutely positive that he wants to talk about curriculum. Margie, surely you don't believe that. Are you deaf, dumb and blind? He looks at you like he could just eat you up."

"Maryleen, don't you ever say anything like that again! I can't believe you would say such a thing. He observes all of us and is a very fair-minded, upstanding gentleman that knows his job and does it impeccably."

"Right! Emma! You are the most naïve woman I have ever known. How did you grow to be so old without falling off a bridge into a river and drowning? You must be from another world, or at least another age. Today's modern woman knows and notices the things that men are doing and thinking. Why I can read a man's mind like it was writing on the wall."

"Stop! Maryleen! You are such a romantic and you're reading way too much into this."

~ ~ ~

Dr. Harrall looked especially handsome. There was a winsome kind of air about him. He realized that he was feeling a bit chipper and his mother commented on it as he bade her "Good Evening," upon leaving the house.

"My, Byron, you certainly are dressed up. Got on your "Sunday best," and it's only Wednesday. What in the world could be going on, and you're dining out in the middle of the week. I smell a mouse, I would say rat, but it's probably only a smaller mystery. Could it be a young lady? What do you say to that?'

"I say, Mother, that you are up to your old tricks and are always jumping to conclusions. However, we love you for it. You keep us all encouraged around here, and if it weren't for you, I wouldn't even have a life, much less the children and their lives. I love you more than you know, and if there's anything happening in my life that's important, you will be the first one to know it."

~ ~ ~

"Hello, Emma. So good to see you this evening." Dr. Harrall was somewhat on the formal side at this most ostentatious beginning of the romance of the century.

"Good Evening, Doctor Harrall," Emma very politely responded.

"Oh, please, Emma, call me Byron. We don't need to stand on formalities this evening."

"Well, if you say so," Emma answered. Actually she was thinking *I don't know what to say or what not to say. This is the most awkward situation of my entire life.*

"Shall we walk on to the café," offering his arm to Emma, "I hope this proves to be a delightful evening for you and for me."

What does that mean? I'm so confused. Emma's head was swimming as she took his arm.

"Did you have a pleasant day?" Byron asked as they strolled on down the street.

"Yes, I did, although I must say I was quite taken aback by your note, and I've thought a great deal about it during the day today."

Emma decided to take the "bull by the horns," and see what was happening.

"Is that good or bad, Emma? Were you looking forward to this evening or dreading it? I surely don't want you to feel obligated."

"Thank you, no . . . I don't feel obligated, just surprised."

"I don't blame you. I really took a chance by writing the letter, and I hoped that you weren't - well, I would say, overcome by the intensity of my feelings."

"I don't even know what I think . . . Byron . . . I'm here though . . . that must mean something."

They had reached the café and the maitre de seemed to be expecting them. He ushered them to a lovely table on the edge of the dining room. It was not secluded, but it certainly was private. There was a gardenia lying at what was obviously her place. Margie [*Emma*] took in a big breath as she looked up at Byron and he was looking at her and she smiled as she had never smiled before. It seemed to come from a place that was brand new and mysterious. *What was happening? What was this spell this man was weaving?* He assisted her with her chair and she felt a pleasure she had never felt before. He hadn't touched her, but he was near and it seemed she could sense the pulsing of his heart.

"Emma, would you entertain a small glass of wine before dinner? That is - only if you want to."

"That would be nice but only one." It wasn't her first taste of wine, but that wasn't common fare for the Casey/Wilson household. *Surely one glass of wine won't corrupt me. I'll keep my senses. This is a special evening. Unbelievable!*

As the waiter seemed to just appear from nowhere and at exactly the right time, Byron gave him the wine order as though he had ordered wine everyday of his life. Having finished instructing the waiter, he smiled at Emma and asked her if she was okay.

She said that she was as she lifted the gardenia to her face to allow its fragrance to waft by her nostrils. *Oh, is there anything more wonderful than that fragrance?*

The wine came and was expertly poured. Byron swished the burgundy liquid in his glass and sipped it as he tasted and tested the bouquet. Margie [*Emma*] was impressed. She had never been in the company of such an elegant man. You would never have expected such things had you only encountered Dr. Harrall in the setting of the school.

"Well, Emma, as I said in my letter. I have admired you from afar since the first time I met you. I believe you are one of the finest human beings I have ever had the pleasure of knowing. I also said that I realize that I am older than you and I am a widower with two children," Byron paused.

"I read it all . . . I didn't know what to think . . . it certainly was unexpected. I had no idea."

"That's what I'm talking about. You are so unassuming. You are complete, competent and so considerate of others, you would never be so arrogant as to even expect that you were the center of anyone's attention. That's part of your beauty. I also said that if you would see me and talk with me, I would most readily accept that your response was nothing more than that of a friend. I will accept that and truly understand."

"I can't even speak to that offer . . . I'm so surprised and even confused . . . yes, the word would be confused . . . that I don't know what to think. But, I am willing to think."

"That's enough! I don't require more than that. Just think, and to be quite trite, *think about what you think* and see where this friendship *or more* leads."

The waiter returned to take their order. Byron asked Emma if she would like him to order for her and she said she would. He did with as much aplomb and charm as he had done everything else and still Emma's mind raced even more trying to capture everything that was going on.

~ 33 ~

*"The LORD is close to the brokenhearted; he
rescues those whose spirits are crushed."*
Philippians 3:8

Joshua and Zoe had plans to have lunch together. Joshua
was rather at loose ends since his appointment had fallen
through at Mount Pisgah and Zoe was beginning to notice
his pensive mood. Jason had discussed the whole situation
with Margie Sunday evening after he, Joshua and Pastor
Robertson had visited with Superintendent Owens. Margie
was very disappointed mostly for Joshua's feelings and
shocked at what "the church" can do at any given moment.
She and Jason strongly agreed that Joshua was much better
off not having gone there to do ministry. Zoe would be
relieved, especially since the parsonage was not really up to
an acceptable condition. Really, it was far below what was
acceptable. Margie and Jason had determined to help them
with some minor renovations at least.

"Joshua, I've missed you." Zoe began with her sweet
voice.

"Well, Dear Heart, you know I always miss you. But,
you have to admit that you have been extremely occupied

with your whirlwind of parties and preparations for the wedding. I'm not complaining, just mentioning the obvious."

"I know, I know. It really has been a bit much, but everyone seems to enjoy it even more than I do. I guess people are just surprised and very glad that anyone would even marry me," laughing Zoe waited for a positive response from Joshua.

"Actually, that is quite a surprise – isn't it. I guess I just got tired of being alone."

"Huh! I like that. I expected you to say something a lot more endearing than that."

"I love you, Zoe. How's that? I can't live without you, Zoe! How about that?"

"That's better. Now, let's get on down to the hotel and have some lunch. I'm famished. I've been putting in late nights and early mornings - so much to do."

Joshua led Zoe to a table that was rather secluded. That was not easy in the dining room of the hotel. He just wanted to be out of the direct line of vision, maybe folks wouldn't see them and come over to chat as was the custom in Tampico. They ordered and Joshua said a quick silent prayer and cleared his throat.

"Zoe, I need to bring you up to date on the latest development with my preaching appointment." Joshua paused hoping the next words would be accepted graciously and with as little hurt as possible.

"What's wrong, Joshua? What IS the latest development?"

"It's not going to happen. That's the latest and that's the bottom line. We aren't going there."

"My goodness, why not, is someone else going? Surely they couldn't find a better person that you, Joshua. Why are you – we not going?"

"The congregation, not all of them, but the majority decided that our being step-relation was not acceptable.

They feel that it would be, well, not so good a situation .
. . to explain . . . or come to understand. Hell, Zoe, I don't
know! I'm so frustrated with them, I could do some harm."

"Joshua, that's not like you. I've never heard you cuss
before – what in the world would elicit such an outburst?"

"I'm sorry. I'm just so disappointed in the church. The
very idea that they would allow such misunderstanding
of the facts, such an unjust "judgment" to prevail has just
brought out feelings in me I didn't even know I had."

Zoe reached across the table and took Joshua's hand,
covering it with both of her hands as she looked deeply into
his eyes and spoke with such sincerity and love that Joshua
was stunned. "Joshua, you are the most dedicated, sincere
man that I have ever known. I realize that I am young and
haven't had many years to observe men or women, but I
know in my heart of hearts that God has brought us together
and whatever life brings we will face it together. With God's
help we will prevail."

"Oh, Zoe, My Love, I cannot tell you how much I appreciate your understanding. I had no idea that you were so deep
and . . . well . . . abiding is the word."

"Joshua, you don't have to protect me from life. I have
watched my mother and your father over these years, not a
lot of years, but enough to know that what is it you always
quote, *If God be for us who could be against us.* Joshua, MY
LOVE, God is for us. There's another quote, I don't know if
it's Scripture or not, but I've heard my mother say it forever
and that is *That God hasn't brought us this far to leave us.*"

"Mrs. Casey, soon-to-be, we are secure in our faith and
our future with God leading. I cannot wait to make you
wholly mine . . . at least in this life."

The timing was perfect. Their food arrived and they
looked up and smiled at the young lady that delivered it and
then clasped their hands as Joshua prayed:

Father, what can we say except thank You. Thank You for life. Thank You for health. Thank You for our unknown future, for You, Oh Almighty God, have gone before us and prepared the way. Thank You now for this food and the hands that have prepared it. In Jesus' name. Amen

Zoe added her "amen!" And they looked at each other, smiled and laughed out loud!

After lunch, they went for a buggy ride and enjoyed the countryside and the beauty of God's good earth. With the wedding only three weeks away, Joshua was hoping that Pastor Robertson's plan would work and he could assist him in the ministry in Tampico and the surrounding areas at least until the possible teaching position came to be reality.

When they arrived home, Zoe, in her unpredictable banter rushed through the house looking for her mother and burst forth, when she found her in the kitchen with, "Have you heard, you and Dad have been harboring sinners? We are on the list bound for the first load to – well, the place of fire and brimstone. Sorry! We tried to do better."

Margie turned around from kneading the bread, wiped her hands on her apron and gave Zoe the biggest hug that could ever be, Margie's mind racing with thanksgiving to God for Zoe's joy and imperturbable heart.

~ *34* ~

*"You must remain faithful to what you have
been taught from the beginning. If you do,
you will remain in fellowship with the Son
and with the Father."*
I John 2:24

Byron and Emma had engaged in fascinating conversation during the entire meal. Emma described her past, her family, the hardships that they had endured and especially her admiration for her mother's "grit." Byron countered with the story of his growing up. Their hardships were similar in many ways but of course somewhat different in detail. Their strengths were the same as well. They both had developed exemplar characters. They were able to handle whatever was to be their plight. Their courage and determination were so comparable and they realized that they had a great deal in common.

It was a comfortable and enjoyable evening. It ended with anticipation for their lives to become more and more together than apart. In fact Byron asked Emma to come to family dinner the next Sunday. "Just want you to meet my mother. She is a soldier. I don't know what I would have done had she not been available to step in and *mother* my children."

Emma accepted the invitation with an excited heart and knew that she would also be meeting Byron's children. A lump formed in her throat as she thought about what they would think of her. But, really, why was that so important? After all, if she and Dr. Harrall - Byron, were to be only friends . . . the children shouldn't have any objections to that.

~ ~ ~

As Emma expected, Maryleen was perched on the edge of the overstuffed chair in the lobby of the residence hall, ready to spring at that first sight of Emma's return. Maryleen knew better than to start asking anything in public, but she was literally licking her lips waiting for the first place of privacy that would allow the evening's activities to be discussed.

"Oh, Emma, I have been on pins and needles . . . I cannot tell you how I've suffered for the past three hours. And, I must add, that a three hour dinner is quite suspect. Tell me! Tell me all, before I expire!"

"Maryleen, you take the cake. You are far too excited . . . and I don't know why. I only went to dinner with a friend and associate. We had a wonderful dinner and some pleasant conversation."

"Certainly! A friend and associate . . . a man who wrote you a love letter, practically asking you to be his wife and you brush it off as a *wonderful dinner and some pleasant conversation*. Emma, do you think I'm stupid? In the first place I watched you prepare, I watched you leave, I've seen you return . . . and Emma . . . if you are not a woman in love, then I am a blue-tick-hound."

"A woman in love, you call me? Maryleen, give me some credit. I don't go around throwing my heart out in the open for just any man to come along and sweep me off my feet. I am completely in control of myself, my emotions and my heart!"

"All right, Emma, have it your way. I can wait until you decide to share with your very best friend in the world. I can just suffer in silence until you burst and I'll have to come and pick up the pieces because you won't share . . . Well, tell me one thing, did he ask to meet you for *pleasant conversation* again in the near future?"

"I will answer that, My Very Best/Nosey Friend in the World, and then you have to promise me you will stop this grilling and let me go to bed . . . the answer is . . . and you cannot let out any loud sounds that would call attention to our discussion. Yes, he asked me to dinner on Sunday at his home . . ."

"Oh, I knew it! I knew it! Oh, my Almighty, God in Heaven, Emma, do you know what this means? I don't think you are human, Emmaline Wilson, you are a frozen block of ice in the deep of winter if you don't realize, he's going to ask you to marry him. . . Oh, my goodness, oh, my goodness." By this time Maryleen was dancing, prancing and otherwise about to fly.

"Help us, Jesus!" Emma exclaimed. "My friend is going to have a heart attack and I'm not a doctor."

With that little humorous, but half-serious prayer, Emma escorted Maryleen to the door of her bedroom and gave her a hug and a light peck on her forehead.

Maryleen, just careened along the wall and rolled her eyes.

~ 35 ~

"How joyful are those who fear the LORD –
all who follow his ways! You will enjoy the
fruit of your labor. How joyful and
prosperous you will be!
Psalm 128:1-2

The whole family was tuned up for the wedding of the century. Truly, it was going to be a wonderful affair. Everyone in town or surrounding area was invited. That's the way things were done. There was enough space reserved for the families and since Joshua and Zoe's family was the same – that was a helpful fact. Everyone else was welcome to come when they wanted to and sit where they could. The church would be packed, but the reception would be glorious. That was to be held at the Casey home, yard, grove of trees behind the house, wherever tables and chairs could be arranged. Most of the guests would bring food and generally just a community get together would be the order of the day.

The huge wedding cake, hopefully so that all could have a bit if they so desired, was being baked two days before and kept fresh in the fruit cellar and protected with moist new dish clothes and some ice (which was quite scarce by then).

The lovely array of attendants was, Emma, maid of honor and then Carol Sue, Alvina and Abby as bridesmaids. The men were equally accounted for with Trey, the best man, by virtue of being the oldest brother. And, then Jeremy, Clay, Jacob as groomsmen. What a beautiful array of young people. Margie was beside herself with pride and emotion at such a blessed and fine day of celebration. This grand celebration was not limited to the wedding ceremony, but to the generations that had gone before. Jason's mother and father had lived with a steadfast attitude toward life and family. Margie's dear mother and father had survived the financial panic of 1837 and many more hardships and losses. They were all disappointed that, Martin, who was busily assigned to his doctoring career in the Army could not manage to get away for the event. Martin insisted that Rose make the trip and enjoy the family event. That completed the wedding party with Marilyn Rose and Sally Renee as flower girls and Patrick Eugene along with Barton Casey escorting the flower girls. What a sight to behold. The town, in fact, the county was a "buzz." There was much speculation and great expectations.

The news that Reverend Joshua Casey would not be serving Mount Pisgah Methodist Episcopal Church had made the gossip-lines. But, for the most part the reason that people were aware of was because Joshua would be interning with Pastor Robertson in preparation for his teaching post at Wesley Theological Seminary in Indianapolis.

That was actually coming true. It had only been a few weeks since the great debacle that had blown up in their faces when the church mothers and fathers made their misdirected decision, but Pastor Robertson, being well respected in all the right circles had gone to bat for Joshua. And, it was actually going to happen, come August, just before the seminary term began.

The most remarkable story that was unfolding the week before the wedding was Emma's romance. Maryleen had come home with Emma the day after the Academy had convened for the summer. She wasted no time in dropping the hints, dishing out little tidbits here and there until Margie and Zoe ganged up on Emma to "tell all."

"Honestly, Mother, Maryleen makes too much of anything and everything. It is true that I have been visiting with Dr. Harrall on a social level, but there's nothing to tell you."

"That's not what Maryleen has told us, Emma, and I can't believe that you're not so excited that you could hardly keep still. But, then knowing you, Emma, I realize that it will be private as long as possible and will be down-played when it is announced."

"Well, is that bad, Mother?"

"No, Honey Dear, it's not bad. It's you. That's one of the reasons I love you so and want you to be happy. You deserve to have a wonderful life, a life that is filled with happiness and wonderful companionship in your marriage. I'm just concerned a bit by Dr. Harrall's age and the ages of his children."

"Well, mother, you and Jason nearly had the same age difference and he had five children and Trey was not much younger than you. You made it. You've had a great life with Jason. There's something to be said about a husband being a little older."

"A little older, Emma, but not twenty years."

"Well, there are no wedding bells in the air . . . and I'm enjoying Byron's, I mean Dr. Harrall's company. And, Mother, you'll just have to trust me."

~ ~ ~

The wedding was perfect. The girls, actually young women, were the most beautiful ever, and the young men were absolutely the most handsome that had ever appeared in that part of the world.

The little folks, of course stole the show. Sally Renee was the pacemaker. She took her job of distributing petals very seriously. Never mind that Marilyn Rose, Patrick and Barton's patience was being severely tried as they coaxed, cajoled and did everything but drag her down the aisle. She went so far as to stop, stoop down and turn over or reposition each petal for the first few feet down the aisle. The others were extremely distressed and embarrassed, but the congregation, that could see what was going on, was delighted with the "goings on." The adults' enjoyment was not shared by the other three children.

Pastor Robertson was at his best and everything went off without a hitch. Joshua was beside himself with joy and love and all the things he had been waiting so long to experience. When Zoe appeared at the head of the aisle, he held his breath and thought for a minute he would pass out. Trey pinched his arm and Jeremy just chuckled. Both of them knew what that was like. It hadn't been that long for either one of them.

Jason, father of the bride, was handsome and very composed. He was so proud of all his children. They were all his . . . he thanked God everyday for his good fortune. He worried about all of them and had proudly watched them grow up. Only Abby and Barton to go . . . he could make it . . . with Margie by his side . . . he knew he was a blessed man of all men.

Margie had really allowed herself to be "decked out" with a lovely frock. She thought, if only Aunt Stella and her mother had still been alive, they would have approved of her glorious countenance. *Oh, if only they could be here. I miss them so.*

The festivities were over, the bride and groom off on their honeymoon and all the family just sitting around in total, wonderful exhaustion.

Much to everyone's surprise, Byron Harrall had travelled to be at the wedding. Emma was not surprised. After several weeks of "keeping company," she knew him quite well. He would move heaven and earth to please her and to be at her side. She was glad. It was a good thing. Her mother and Jason were very kind and attentive to Dr. Harrall, as time allowed, and now after all the guests were gone – they could settle down and just be family.

Recounting the day's activities was the order of the evening . . . and the very most important thing for the elder Caseys was getting to know Dr. Harrall. It was so obvious how he felt about Emma. He was so confident, but humble. He was very attentive but also reserved. He didn't seem to have an arrogant bone in his body. He was so honest and forthright. You couldn't help but respect Byron Harrall and really hope at the same time that you could be around him more.

Margie could see that "it," Emma and Byron, was to be. She approached the evening and its conversation with a grace that Jason certainly knew her to have and Byron recognized as the same charm and grace that Emma possessed.

The family was pleased that Emma and Byron had found each other. They made a wonderful and gracious couple and were married later that year. Time would prove their love for each other and their families. God's hand was at work.

~ 36 ~

*"I took my troubles to the LORD;
I cried out to him, and he answered my prayer."*
Psalm 120:1

~ Winter of 1878 ~

The battle for the west was still raging as the government was trying hard to squelch the activities of the Native Americans. The U.S. Army began to capture the horses that provided mobility to the Comanche Indians. Quanah Parker, who was the last great Comanche chief, finally surrendered.

George was still extremely interested in the welfare and events that surrounded the Indians. He researched, wrote letters and generally made a nuisance of himself with Martin's connections with the Army. He found that Quanah Parker was born of a white woman who had been captured in 1836 by the Comanches when she was only nine. She was adopted into the Nocona Band of Comanches. She later married the son of a tribal chief and had two more children. She was found and rescued in a raid and returned to her white family. She wanted to be reunited with those whom she considered "her people," her Indian Family. That was not to be, and she starved herself to death within a few years.

George was particularly adept at ferreting out details and writing interesting stories for the local and national newspapers. One of his favorites was the transition of a religious movement that was taking shape in that same year. General William Booth, the founder of The Salvation Army was leading the charge in reform with a military like religious organization that was causing a lot of controversy and speculation in the lives of the religious.

Joshua was particularly interested in George's research especially in regard to the forming of The Salvation Army. When he was in the midst of his studies in seminary, he had written numerous papers on the plight of those who were considered the "down and out." He has always taken to heart Jesus' words of seeking the least, the last and the lost. He knew and taught that religion was not just for the privileged. After all hadn't John and Charles Wesley proven that less than a century ago when they had reached out to those who were the forgotten.

Actually, the work of the Wesleys had averted a bloody revolution that would have taken England just like the French Revolution scarred the people and the history of France. As many as 40,000 people were killed in France during the years of siege, and it was primarily based on the "haves" versus the "have nots." The Wesleys dealt with educating and supporting the common people in England during a time when poverty and rebellion against the establishment was at its height.

Joshua realized what a gift that was given through the teachings of Jesus when he asks his followers why they didn't take care of him when he was in need. The Gospel of Matthew chapter 25 is the premise for Jesus' teachings:

"But when the Son of Man comes in his glory,
and all the angels with him, then he will sit upon
his glorious throne. All the nations will be gathered
in his presence, and he will separate the people as
a shepherd separates the sheep from the goats. He
will place the sheep at his right hand and the goats
at his left. "Then the King will say to those on his
right, 'Come, you who are blessed by my Father,
inherit the Kingdom prepared for you from the
creation of the world. For I was hungry, and you fed
me. I was thirsty, and you gave me a drink. I was a
stranger, and you invited me into your home. I was
naked, and you gave me clothing. I was sick, and
you cared for me. I was in prison, and you visited
me.' "Then these righteous ones will reply, 'Lord,
when did we ever see you hungry and feed you?
Or thirsty and give you something to drink? Or a
stranger and show you hospitality? Or naked and
give you clothing? When did we ever see you sick or
in prison and visit you?' "And the King will say, 'I
tell you the truth, when you did it to one of the least
of these my brothers and sisters, you
were doing it to me."

Joshua had thought on this for many years and knew
that it would be a central part of his theology and preaching.
Little did he suspect the hardship through death and disease
that would be wrought on him and his.

~ *37* ~

*"Direct your children onto the right path, and
when they are older, they will not leave it."*
Proverbs 22:6

The Casey/Wilson/Smallwood clan was busy with life
in their various venues. Trey and Carol Sue had given
birth to their second child, a little boy. Alvina and Jeremy
were busy tending to twins. The girls had been born in late
December of 1876, and were doing well. Margie was on
the scene and "grand mothering" all over the place between
three newly arrived grandchildren within six months of
each other. Reverend (almost Doctor) Joshua Casey and his
lovely, but not so happy young wife, Zoe were struggling in
Indianapolis to keep body and soul together. Joshua realized
that the ministry or teaching would not be very lucrative, but
he had no idea how "little" little was. Zoe tried to cope. They
had received a bundle from heaven as well, but were too far
away from grandparents to have much if any help.

Their best support came from Emma and Byron who had
married almost 18 months ago. Byron continued in his role as
Head Master of the American Academy. Emma split her time
between mothering Phillip and Laura, who were now almost
fifteen and ten. Additionally, Emma taught several classes

a week at the Academy. Her most cherished time was spent with the children, teaching and helping them grow into the fine people that she knew they would become. Being loved by Byron was the center of her life . . . she could never have imagined such love. Byron's mother was "all" that Byron had described her to be. She loved Emma like a daughter. Contrary to mother-in-law stories, she delighted in her son's marriage and her new daughter-in-law's gifts and talents.

Jacob had been given an opportunity to become a personal tutor for the children of a very wealthy family and was traveling and living in Europe with the family most of the time. Abby, Clay and Barton were still at home. Clay was working in the store and trying his hand at some writing, taking after Grandfather George. Abby was close to finishing the educational opportunities in Tampico and Barton . . . well, Barton was busy, busier and busiest.

Everyone was doing their best to make good on all counts. Zoe was the one, out of all of them, that was finding life difficult. She had gotten pregnant within the first year of their marriage and was not too happy with the condition. She would rather have been hosting parties and planning her next shopping trip. George Alexander, the darling little boy that had been sent to their family was a happy baby and easy to manage. He seemed to be doing well enough, but with the winter winds and the influenza outbreaks, Zoe was always worried about him. He did seem to have a pervasive cough that came about more and more often.

Joshua reminded her every day, not to worry. She didn't have to go out in the cold. Actually, their little apartment was almost as cold as the outside. Everyone was suffering that winter. It had come on so suddenly and stayed without much relief.

Zoe awakened in the middle of the night at the sound of her worst fear . . . the baby was sick. He had a racking, croupy cough that seemed like choking instead of breathing.

She rushed to the crib to find Baby George in a fit of coughs that sounded like a dog barking. He couldn't seem to get his breath.

Doctors had called the condition the "croup." It was actually an obstructive condition of the larynx or trachea occurring chiefly in infants and children. The obstruction could be caused by allergy, a foreign body, infection, or a tumor.

No matter what was the cause the condition was almost as debilitating for the parents as it was the child. You would hold your breath and gasp for breath yourself, hoping that the child would be able to catch its next breath.

Zoe wakened Joshua and retrieved the baby from his crib. She knew to put a kettle or pot to boiling and make a tent for the steam to hopefully relieve some of the congestion and eliminate the choking cough.

"Joshua, hurry. He's choking to death."

"Zoe, stay calm . . . I'm stoking the fire in the stove . . . it will take a few minutes for the water to boil. Let's pray, Zoe, we need peace and calm . . . that will do the baby more good than anything."

"Well, if he isn't better in a bit . . . you have to go for the doctor."

"Honey, the doctor has told us before that he sounds a lot worse than he actually is. Just stay calm and pray."

"Pray? Pray! Joshua, do you really think God cares? If God cared babies wouldn't get sick like this."

"That's not true, Zoe, God knows and is here with us. The world is the sickness . . . the world and its selfish, devil may care attitude is what causes much of the suffering. And, besides that the Word of God tells us to count it all joy when we suffer."

"Oh, God in heaven, Joshua! You are an idiot. Are you joyful now that your son can't get his breath? Are you joyful, Joshua, that your wife is about to have a heart attack worrying over your son?"

Ignoring Zoe's unkind remarks, Joshua, arranged the newspaper around the pot to channel the steam for the baby's ease of breathing. "Here, Zoe, bring the baby to me. I'll sit with him in this steam – he'll be fine in a minute."

Zoe gladly handed little George over to his daddy. Then she could pace more strongly, wringing her hands and muttering to herself. Where had Zoe inherited this extreme impatience? How had she managed to reach her adult life and not have any more sense or sense of calmness than she had?

Margie had often worried about Zoe's lack of patience and her almost pathological bent toward anger and escape. Margie had prayed and hoped that the characteristics that Zoe seemed to have inherited from her father would disappear as she matured. Margie had studied the Bible references to the "sins of the generations." She wondered what sins, which generation? How could children be so different? Emma had the patience of a saint. Clay was quiet and not too forthcoming, but he certainly didn't have the tyrannical attitude about life that his twin, Zoe, had.

"I'm going for Emma. I'll get dressed and go get her."

"Zoe, it's two o'clock in the morning. How in the world do you think that you're going to get way out on Illinois Avenue at this hour? It's not safe . . . you'll freeze before you get there and what can Emma do that we're not doing?"

"Oh, God, Joshua, I just can't stand it. I can't just stand by and wait. I have to do something."

"Well, get on your knees and pray. Ask God to give you some sense."

"Huh! Is that what you tell your students . . . pray for sense. If we had more cents and dollars we wouldn't be in this God-forsaken flat, walking the floor in the middle of the night asking a God who obviously doesn't care to give us SENSE! We wouldn't be freezing to death day and night with the wind coming in around the windows and your breath hanging in the air like icicles in the middle of the night."

Morning finally came . . . Joshua found one of the street people to take messages to the seminary and to Emma. He couldn't leave Zoe alone. When they finally got the baby settled . . . Zoe didn't sleep even then. Hopefully, Emma can come. She is the best medicine.

The morning wore on and finally Zoe heard the familiar rap on their door. Emma stuck her head in the door as she called out, "Hello, help has arrived from the fort. Where are you folks? Brought some freshly baked cinnamon rolls . . . who's for a cup of tea?"

"Oh, Emma, I'm so glad you're here. I wanted to come and get you last night . . ."

"Yes, at two in the morning . . . she was coming . . .," Joshua piped up.

"I'm so sorry, Zoe, you must have been frantic. How's the baby now?"

"He's resting, but it probably won't be for long. I know he's feverish. He ate a little . . . then I finally rocked him to sleep. Listen to him breathe, Emma, he sounds like a steam engine, wheezing and straining."

"The doctor is coming by after lunch," Joshua offered, "I'm sure tonight will be much better."

Emma stepped into the kitchen area and realized that there was a lot to be done there. She took off her coat and found an apron.

Zoe was aware that Emma was probably doing "something" and she called out to her, "Emma, don't do that . . . I'll get to it later."

"You get some rest, Miss Zoe, will the baby sleeps. You too, Joshua, I'll listen for him. I've had a good night's rest."

The next hour was fairly uneventful. The knock on the door was light and Emma rushed to let the doctor in. Everything took on a different sound with the doctor, moving around and it woke the baby. "Let's see here . . . what's happening here, young man?" The doctor bent over the crib.

By this time, the baby was fussing. "Hummmm . . . pretty warm . . . is he taking any fluid?"

"Yes, a little . . . he just doesn't seem to be interested in anything," Zoe responded.

"Let me see here . . . let's listen to these lungs . . .," the doctor proceeded.

Emma already knew that Baby George was more serious than either Joshua or Zoe knew.

Emma had a sixth sense, an understanding if you will, about what is right in a situation and what is not. She could tell by the baby's pallor and his general appearance that he was indeed very ill.

"Mother," Dr. Cunningham was speaking to Zoe, "your baby is burning up with fever, and his lungs are in trouble."

"What do you mean, Doctor?" Zoe almost demanded. "That couldn't be, he only became ill last night. He couldn't be, as you say, in trouble. No! That's not true."

By the time Joshua had moved toward Zoe and was standing at her side.

The doctor then addressed Joshua, "Rev. Casey, your baby has pneumonia. Both of his lungs are affected and unless his fever breaks and something like a miracle happens, he will not make it."

"No! No!" Zoe screamed. Joshua took her by the shoulders and turned her around to embrace her and hold her up.

Emma stepped up and lifted the baby from the crib to redress him. He was burning up with fever. She tried to quiet him, but that wasn't happening. The poor, little thing was gasping for breath, coughing and nearly choking on each breath.

The doctor turned to Emma, "Here is some salve you might rub on his chest. It might calm him down and make it easier for him to breathe. You can continue the steam treatments and keep him wrapped up so that he doesn't take a chill. I'll be back before bedtime to see how you're doing."

With that string of instructions, he headed for the door. Joshua let go of Zoe to follow him and stepped out in the hall with him. "Doctor, wait, he is going to be all right, isn't he?"

Joshua was pleading for an affirmative answer.

"I can't say, Rev. Casey. These cases are hard to predict. I have at least twelve patients with the same situation right now, three elderly and nine children or babies. He is among the sickest I have seen. I know it comes on very quickly and there just isn't much we can do, but wait and hope and pray that he will be strong enough to fight it off. I'll be back later."

Joshua stood in the hall staring after the doctor as he descended the stairs . . . *Hope and pray that he is strong enough? How could he be so sick so suddenly? He seemed to be fine when we put him to bed. I don't know what to do.*

Emma called Joshua from the doorway to come in and help her with Zoe. She had laid the baby back in the crib and was trying to keep Zoe in some semblance of sanity. It wasn't working. Zoe had become frantic. She was sobbing and moaning, rocking back and forth as she sat on the floor.

Joshua half lifted her and got her up on her feet, then picked her up and carried her to the bed. "Emma, can you stay? I need to see if I can stop the doctor and get something for Zoe. We can't manage her like this and take care of the baby too."

"Of course I can stay, Joshua. You go on . . . see what the doctor will give you for Zoe."

They were able to sedate Zoe and Joshua and Emma took turns walking the floor and trying to soothe Baby George. He was trying hard to breathe in between wracking coughs. They tried the steam, they applied the salve . . . Emma tried giving him teaspoons of cold water. Nothing seemed to help. Finally the doctor got back in the late evening.

"Oh, thank God, you're here, Dr. Cunningham. We haven't been able to quiet him at all. He has struggled all afternoon."

"Well, as I said, unless his fever breaks, he won't improve. Let me give a listen to these lungs." Doctor Cunningham shook his head and closed his eyes for a moment.

"Why don't we take him to the hospital, doctor?"

"That wouldn't do any good, Rev. Casey, it won't help him. There are many cases just like him there and you're doing all that you can. If he makes it through the night, chances are he will survive. Pray, Rev. Casey, pray!"

Emma stood at the end of the crib and tried her best to soothe the little guy. He was worn out. Emma prayed.

The elderly and the very young were at the mercy of this horrible killer. George Alexander Casey breathed his last around three a.m. Zoe was awake, but totally not present. She didn't even cry. She held the baby when he finally stopped breathing and wouldn't let Joshua take him. Emma finally sat by her and helped her hold him until she let go and collapsed where she sat. Joshua embraced her and held her tightly while Emma stood to gently lay the baby in his crib. The tears slid down Emma's cheeks, but she didn't make a sound. She could hear Joshua reciting the 23rd Psalm and she knew that Zoe didn't hear a word. George Alexander Casey had gone to be with the Lord. It was not what anyone expects to have happen or thinks that they could live through it.

Even though I walk through the valley of the shadow of death, the Lord is with me.

~ *38* ~

"The LORD is close to the brokenhearted;
he rescues those whose spirits are crushed."
Psalm 34:18

The church was filled with family and friends. Pastor Robertson's voice filled the void. Presiding over a service of a child is one of the hardest things that a pastor ever has to face. Pastor Robertson's life had been so entwined with that of Joshua and Zoe, and now he was saying the final words over their firstborn.

Suffer the little ones to come unto me and forbid them not, for of such is the kingdom of God.

Zoe was practically in the casket as well. She had hardly slept since that fateful night. It seemed like a lifetime, but it was only two days ago. Laudanum had worked for a while, but she couldn't take it in doses that would actually help her because then she wouldn't eat or drink. Renee had stayed at the house with her and the rest of the family were at the church with Joshua.

It was hard to gather 'round Zoe and Joshua as family as the other young folks had their healthy babies in tow. Trey and Carol Sue, Jeremy and Alvina had their little ones and it was just too much for all of them. Margie was her faithful, grace-filled self. She took care of Zoe with care and patience. Joshua was doing as well as could be expected. Emma had not left Zoe's side and Byron stood at the ready by Emma's side.

It was a sad and difficult time.

~ ~ ~

Jason was sitting in the parlor with Joshua. Joshua hadn't said much in the past three days to anyone. He seemed to be comfortable sitting with his father and he finally spoke, "Father, I know that George Alexander is at home with the Lord, but I really don't understand why . . . I don't expect you to know either, but I have to talk to somebody."

"Well, son, you can talk to me anytime. I'm always available. And, you're right I don't know and I can't answer you. I can only call on my memories of such deep and devastating loss in the deaths of my parents. Of course as I recall your mother's passing, I can begin to relate. I guess when your mother died and dear, little Abigail was left motherless, I had my job cut out for me. I had to live and "do" what needed to be done for all the rest of you."

"I am so worried about Zoe. I can't reach her. She is in a place all by herself," Joshua's voice broke as he cried for the first time since the baby's death.

Jason moved over to the settee to comfort Joshua. He put his arm around Joshua's shoulders and bowed his head to offer a silent prayer from his heart. Jason couldn't even bring himself to pray aloud. What to say? What to pray especially to a pastor.

The wonderful passage from Romans came to his mind and he gave thanks. Chapter eight, verses 26-28:

*In the same way, the Spirit helps us in our
weakness. We do not know what we ought to pray
for, but the Spirit himself intercedes for us with
groans that words cannot express. And he who
searches our hearts knows the mind of the Spirit,
because the Spirit intercedes for the saints in
accordance with God's will.*

Joshua brought himself under control, or maybe it was his father's silent prayers, because he felt a surge of peace and he accepted the handkerchief his dad offered him. He wiped his eyes. A faint smile crept across his face as he turned to his father and they stood to have a father-son embrace.

"Do you feel like eating a bite, son? Your mother has some hot soup and I think I saw some food still out on the kitchen table. In fact there is so much food – it would take an army to do it justice."

"Sure, Dad, I'll eat a bite. I have work ahead of me that will take all the strength I can muster and all that God will lend me."

The men moved toward the kitchen when they heard a terrifying scream from the upstairs. Zoe was succumbing once again to her terror and her inconsolable pain. Joshua turned around and slowly climbed the stairs to see what he could do.

Emma was holding Zoe in her arms on the edge of the bed and Margie was praying. There was nothing else to do. The women, sister and mother were giving all that they had and praying that God would supply the rest.

Joshua entered the room and Zoe looked up at him and ran to him sobbing as she fell into his arms, "Oh, Joshua, Joshua our baby is dead! What did we do wrong? What did I do wrong? Why had God done this to us?"

"My Dear . . . Pastor Robertson told us that God's heart is broken too. This world is a fallen place. God is with us and he will see us through this horrible time, but we have to allow God to do that."

Margie and Emma slipped out of the room and left Joshua to comfort Zoe. At least she was talking. She seemed to be back from her dark place. They knew that Joshua was her greatest comfort, and they stopped to pray together outside the door.

~ ~ ~

Joshua and Zoe stayed two weeks at home with their family. Zoe mostly kept herself confined to their room. Joshua visited with Pastor Robertson on a daily basis and was growing stronger by the day. Zoe was beginning to eat and function in a somewhat natural order. She had lost a great deal of weight over those two weeks, but she was becoming herself more and more as each day passed.

Pastor Robertson encouraged Joshua to return to work, and he wanted to. Zoe was not able to even talk about returning to anything. It seemed she was barely surviving with her mother's care. It was decided that she would remain in Tampico and Joshua would go back to his position at the seminary. Emma and Byron invited Joshua to move in with them. They had plenty of room and he would be surrounded by family. Trey and Jeremy helped Emma move Zoe and Joshua's things to the Harralls and Joshua was back to class by the beginning of the third week after Baby George's death.

His students and the faculty were more than kind. Joshua was a strong example to them all even though he had lost a great deal of his life and identity as a father. He understood why Zoe was so devastated, but he also knew that he had to accept reality, exercise his faith in God and continue to live. He kept recalling the scripture from Deuteronomy that talks about life:

*This day I call heaven and earth as witnesses
against you that I have set before you life and death,
blessings and curses. Now choose life, so that you
and your children may live and that you may love
the Lord your God, listen to his voice and hold fast
to him. For the Lord is your life.* (Deut. 30:19-20a)

A good word – and yet – a hard word, his child had not lived. Where is God in that? Pastor Robertson had explained that many things happen in this life, as we know it, that are not our choice. Things that are so painful that you cannot help but wonder how could a good and gracious God allow such. However, as he continued to teach and lead Joshua in the beginning of new understanding Joshua began to accept the insight that *it is not yet time*. Not yet time for perfection.

"Yes, Joshua, our children leave us, our lives become very difficult in many ways, people make bad choices every day. God is not surprised. God is sovereign, yet this life is not all there is. It not yet time for perfection." Pastor Robertson had many years of experience and nurturing, leading families through this horrendous pain.

That phrase, "not yet time for perfection," seemed to be the most comforting thing that Joshua could concentrate on – that and the wonderful passage from Psalm 139 about God knowing us even before we were born. GOD KNOWS US BEFORE WE ARE BORN! What a comfort and strength that is if we will only believe it and receive it. .

*For you created my inmost being; you knit me
together in my mother's womb. I praise you because
I am fearfully and wonderfully made; your works
are wonderful, I know that full well. My frame was
not hidden from you when I was made in
the secret place.*

Byron and Emma were the support that Joshua needed. Not too much sympathy and yet deep understanding and care. Joshua enjoyed the Harrall children. They were young adults now.

Andrew, who was almost sixteen had a mind of his own and was always ready to discuss anything with Joshua that he could. He especially wanted to talk about God and how to think of Him. Joshua well knew those questions. He had them himself at that age. Actually, Joshua found himself filling the role for Andrew that Pastor Robertson had filled for him.

~ 39 ~

"The Lord gives power to the weak and strength to the powerless. Even youths will become weak and tired, and young men will fall in exhaustion. But those who trust in the LORD will find new strength. They will soar high on wings like eagles. They will run and not grow weary. They will walk and not faint."
Isaiah 40:29-31

Margie knew instinctively what to do to help Zoe the most. She insisted that Zoe help around the house, but most importantly that she should return to her music. She asked her to teach, to encourage and even, maybe form a mini-class of Music Appreciation for Abby and Bart. Margie masterminded the whole arrangement with explaining to Abby that she, being a young adult, could be the assistant. If Zoe was to take on children Bart's age, Zoe would need lots of help.

All in all there were three girls and two boys, ages five to eight. *Whew!* It was heavenly work though. God was in it. Zoe rose to the occasion without even realizing that this was the healing balm for her. Her music had always been the strength of her personality.

The class met at the church after school on Tuesdays and Thursdays. Of course, Pastor Robertson was in on the whole plan. There would have been more children, but not to overwhelm Zoe was the best plan. They studied theory and history and of course voice and harmonization – at quite a beginning level. One little boy was particularly attracted to the piano and Zoe took him on as a private piano student.

Joshua managed to get back and forth almost every week-end. The Academy and the college were able to arrange his schedule so that he had no Monday classes, giving him a three day week-end. The trip from Indianapolis only took three hours by train but the before and after time of the trip stretched the length of travel to almost six hours in all.

Zoe was gaining strength every day, and by the end of the school term, she was regaining her health and mental outlook. Zoe had been allowed to stay in a state of childishness even into and after Baby George's birth and death. Emma, the big sister, had coddled her as a child and Zoe had soaked it up and insisted on more. Life had then swamped her with harsh realities of hard, work, pain and inexplicable loss.

The Music Class was planning a mini-concert just before school was out and Zoe was very excited. Abby had prevailed as the "star" of the class. Not only had she learned a great deal in the short four months, but she had really helped with the development and interest of several of the children. She was playing a simple piano duet with one of the little girls. She was also playing a piano solo and singing a duet with Zoe. It turned out to be a grand affair on a Sunday Evening complete with punch and cookies. Margie saw to that.

Joshua was bursting with pride in Zoe's accomplishments and recovery. They would live again – God is faithful – if we will only try. Speaking of trying – or even not trying – Zoe had something to tell Joshua on this very auspicious week-end.

"Joshua, Darling, I hope you are as thrilled as I am – I know you will be!"

"What, Zoe, what are you talking about? The concert? Yes, I'm thrilled. You are a magician to get all that music out of those little people, especially Bart."

"Well, thank you kind, sir. The THRILL though is ours and ours alone. Doctor Cummings says probably a Christmas present."

"Zoe, Doctor Cummings . . . what? Oh, Zoe, you mean . . . ??"

"That's exactly what I mean," Zoe nearly in tears – of joy – grinning from ear to ear.

Joshua hugged, lifted, squeezed and cried all at the same time. "Oh, Zoe, My Love, how wonderful. Who knows?"

"Well, just my mother. I swore her to secrecy, but she had even guessed it before I went to the doctor. You know that wonderful visitor in the morning. Not quite as sick as I was with Baby George, but I know that sign well."

"Christmas present, you say. . . hummmm . . . then only five or six months to go. Guess I'd better get busy finding us a place to live and raise this young lady or gentleman. Zoe, I couldn't be happier. In fact, I'm overjoyed. Let's celebrate. I'm taking you out, young lady. How about a date at the new restaurant in town? That is if you can eat in the evening."

"Oh, I can eat. I eat all the time . . . it's just keeping it in me . . . that's the trick."

Zoe was practically her old self. Joshua was delighted and also cautious. The past five months, well, actually the past three years had been precarious – to say the least. While Zoe was a strong personality – she wasn't always so strong in her character. The recovery from the loss of George Alexander, as well as the pregnancy and his birth, were at the least difficult and often almost more than Joshua thought he could bear.

Zoe loved life as long as *life loved her* and it went "her way." The testing of her mettle was a test for those who loved her. Joshua wanted to broach the subject of moving Zoe away from her mother and extended family.

"*Zoe*, you know I love you more than my own life. I want you to be happy. I consider that among the most important goal in my life, but along with seeing you happy in life is that of answering the "call from God.""

"Joshua, what are you getting at . . . you are about to tell me what?"

"Well, we may need to move in order for me to work at my call and support our family."

"Move? Move where, Joshua? What are you talking about?"

"Pastor Robertson and I have been in consultation about my ministry, what that looks like, how that might be lived out."

"And . . . ?" Zoe was always rushing ahead to get to the bottom line. Everyone knew her anxiety and hoped she would like the "bottom line."

"And, I believe I could have an appointment this June. We would move into the parish to become the Pastor's Family for a church and community."

Zoe reached across the table and placed her hand over Joshua's, "Joshua, you are the dearest and most loving man I have ever known. I know that God has called you to minister to his flock. I think I am called too – that is to walk along side you."

It was almost the same setting, and the same intimate, sincere speech that Zoe had spoken to Joshua nearly three years ago. He had taken her to lunch just before their marriage to explain why Mount Pisgah Church did not want them. She defended him then. She encouraged him now.

"Oh, Zoe, how could I be so lucky. After what all we've been through with the church, I wasn't sure you would be able . . . or willing to try it again."

"Joshua, as I told you then, I'll tell you again . . . whatever life brings . . . and I pray that it's happy and healthy, with God's help we will prevail. I love you. I know that you love me with an everlasting and wonderful love. You put up with me . . . don't you?"

Zoe smiled and Joshua leaned over and kissed her – on the lips – in public – and neither one of them cared what people might think.

~ 40 ~

"Let your roots grow down into him, and let your lives be built on him. Then your faith will grow strong in the truth you were taught, and you will overflow with thankfulness."
(Colossians 2:7)

Thanksgiving came and went. Jacob managed to get home. He was burdened with gifts of perfume, silk scarves, picture postcards and anything else he could bring home from Europe. The family he travelled with, as tutor, spared no cost to continually be in motion. There wasn't a museum, a concert, a palace, or a fancy hotel that was safe from their presence. You name it, they were there. Jacob, the humble soul that he was, took it in stride.

He loved his family more than anything he had ever done or any place he had ever been.

Keeping up with his nieces and nephews was his biggest challenge and joy, not to mention his little prodigy – the Brother Bart, who absolutely idolized Jacob. But, then everybody loved Jacob.

Joshua had been in touch with Pastor Robertson and the Bishop of the Indiana Conference of the Episcopal Methodist Church. He was to be appointed. This time there would not be any of the nonsense and ridicule that they had suffered with Mount Pisgah Church.

This appointment would be north of Indianapolis, spreading the family out in a northerly direction, but it was a good and stable congregation and they were more than pleased with the prospect of having Doctor Joshua Casey and Mrs. Casey. They understood that they had a "twofer" as well. That is the title given to a pastor-couple where the wife brings extra gifts to the congregation. Zoe's musical ability was indeed as great a gift to the congregation as Joshua's education and skill in pastoring. It works both ways. Zoe needed the support and appreciation that it would bring her as well.

The move was to be as soon as possible. The church had been without a pastor for several months. The whole family was involved in the task. That is the whole family that was available. Mostly the men and Margie and Emma were the most helpful to be had. The parsonage was acceptable. It was in much better condition than what Mount Pisgah offered.

Zoe was four months plus in her pregnancy, and of course while she was perfectly fit and willing to work with the best of them. Her mother insisted that she supervise and supervise she did. The good people from Marion Episcopal Methodist Church turned out on the day the entourage arrived in town and it was a great blessing. The women of the congregation had planned the food for the day and the next day. The men showed up in numbers to assist with the moving, a wonderful beginning for the new pastor and his wife with child. The women were particularly excited about a new baby in the parsonage. It had been a long time since that had happened.

Trey and Jeremy started back to Tampico with the wagons the next morning. Jason, Margie, Abby and Emma stayed at the local hotel. Byron, regretfully, had to stay near the centers of learning he supported. The end of the fall term demanded his presence.

Margie, Abby and Emma were back at the parsonage early the next morning to help Zoe get settled. The house had been freshened by the ladies of the church. Things were happening for the good of all. Jason took the time to nose around Marion to see what was going on in the local fare of business. That's what made Jason so successful as a merchant. He paid attention.

~ ~ ~

The dust, if there was any dust, had settled by Wednesday and the family had all headed south. Dr. Joshua was working on his first sermon and Zoe was enjoying the piddling. Zoe was doing all the little things than women do to make a house a home. There were three bedrooms. The overall appearance of the parsonage was modest, but it was roomy. The second and third bedrooms afforded a nursery for the new arrival and a study for Joshua. The church had managed to secure a piano for Zoe and the parsonage was complete.

Sunday came quickly and everyone was poised to listen, observe and give their opinions.

Joshua preached on the Great Commission, Matthew chapter 28. He talked about what Jesus told his followers before he left this earth, and that was to "Go, Make Disciples, Teach and Baptize." He honed in on "authority" that Jesus had and gave to his disciples, making the point that as believers in Jesus Christ we are all under "discipline" and are disciples with authority. It went over well. There were several "amens," and everyone, even the children, gave rapt attention.

There was a covered dish dinner immediately following the service. It was well furnished and well attended. Zoe was in her element. She loved attention and always made a great effort to notice everyone and invite them into her life. The "folks of the church" conferred later that day and all during the next week that they had been doubly blessed. They loved and appreciated Joshua and Zoe from the beginning.

The Marion M.E. Church was comprised of the more affluent families of the area, but they were more than willing to evangelize. The Wednesday night Board Meeting was directed in that vein. The chairman of the board, Dr. Aaron Huckaby, was the leading doctor of Marion. He had been born and raised in a missionary family. His father, Dr. Samuel Huckaby, had been a medical doctor and a missionary in New Zealand in the early 1800's. Aaron was born in Ruatara, New Zealand, where the Reverend Samuel Marsden had been working with the Maori people.

The elder Dr. Huckaby and his wife were among the first to prepare for missions even before the "call" was issued to folks with medical backgrounds. They returned to England just before their second child was born and eventually migrated to the colonies in America. They then moved westward with the "call of the west" to settle the vast country. Many churches in the new territory could claim their beginnings from the Huckabys.

Dr. Huckaby was a colorful and interesting man. He was entirely dedicated to the church and her mission, so he was thrilled with Joshua's fervor and bent toward preaching the gospel. He was particularly interested in the newly developing China Inland Mission.

The non-sectarian China Inland Mission was founded on principles of faith and prayer. From the beginning it recruited missionaries from the working class as well as single women. Dr. and Mrs. Huckaby's oldest daughter was even then preparing to go to China with the Inland Mission, so there was no getting around what the tenor of the church in Marion was about.

~ ~ ~

Zoe was very proud of her dear husband and his work in the church. She had formed a children's choir soon after their arrival and she sang solos in worship when called upon. It was not entirely appropriate for women who were "with child," to be on public display, but she did it anyway. That was Zoe. If Joshua wasn't put off by it, then she reasoned no one should be.

It caused some "behind the hand" conversation, especially among the women. However, generally it was overlooked since Zoe was so young and ambitious. They didn't want to squelch her attributes and gifts. The pastors that had been serving the church for the past twenty years were rather stodgy and their wives did as little as possible. Modern thinking was becoming the order of the day.

Thanksgiving came and went. The church joined in the community celebration and Dr. Joshua Casey, the "new kid on the block," was asked to bring the message. He presented the traditional founding of this new and exciting country through the faith of the forefathers and mothers. It was an interesting sermon with much drama reminding the community who these people were and what was expected of this new and promising land.

Zoe was asked to bring her children's choir and they were received with great appreciation and admiration. The Marion Methodist Episcopal Church was fast becoming the "happening" place of Marion.

Christmas was approaching and so was the birth of the baby. Dr. Huckaby had suggested a young doctor who was then practicing in town as the attending physician and Zoe was delighted. Dr. Huckaby didn't come right out and say it, but he intimated that the new doctor had been schooled in the latest techniques and possible complications of childbirth.

Actually, Zoe was relieved that she wouldn't be attended by someone she sang to and socialized with on a weekly basis.

Jason and Margie were traveling north to be near when the birth occurred and had just arrived three days before Zoe went into labor. It was December the 21st. Ida Emmaline Casey was born, crying at the top of her lungs. She weighed nine pounds even and had a full head of black hair. Everyone was delighted. Zoe had weathered this second pregnancy with much more ease and understanding and acceptance of what was happening. Her labor and delivery was normal and all was well with the world.

Ida Emmaline was baptized the second Sunday after her birth with her grandparents, Aunt Abby and Uncle Barton present. Her daddy was the officiate. The congregation was pleased and excited. Emma and Byron had come north for Christmas and stayed on through New Year's and the baptism. Byron was not due back until Christmas vacation was over.

~ 41 ~

"We must listen very carefully to the truth we have heard, or we may drift away from it."
Hebrews 2:1

~ 15 Years Later ~

The spring of 1895 dawned. The past fifteen years had produced four daughters in the Casey family. Ida Emmaline who was dubbed "Emmy" by the family and Amanda Belle, who was named for Joshua's mother and Zoe's great aunt. She was born two years after Ida Emmaline. Amanda was Amanda Belle, the full "title." Her "title" fit her perfectly in size and determination. She was a mini-Zoe in the flesh. She was born in charge and demanded attention. So, Amanda Belle was not too much to say in addressing this young dynamo.

Grethel Gertrude and Jesse Vanell had come along after a wide space of almost ten years between the first two girls and the second two girls. Greth, as she was fondly called, was born in February of 1890 and Jesse Vanell was born in the same month of 1891.

Joshua and Zoe were disappointed that Emmy and Amanda Belle had not been blessed with brothers or sisters.

However, after ten years, they were quite surprised by the discovery that Zoe was going to have another child. She was thrilled. She didn't feel she was too old, after all she was only thirty-three. People made too much of having your children young. She had been through that, and the loss of Baby George at such an early age still haunted her. George Alexander Casey would have been almost fifteen years old had he lived.

Grandfather George was past eighty and the family hovered over him like he was a saint. Actually, he was. He had been through much in his lifetime, the loss of his young sweetheart, Emma, and before that Barton's death, Martin's twin, at only age five. George had lived through the death and destruction of the Civil War. He had seen Martin, the young and brave doctor, healed from his addiction while serving as a healer in the war to end all wars. Then he had to helplessly stand by when Zoe suffered the death of her first-born. His Renee had been his strength. She still continued to be just that. George and Renee had found their place in Tampico. Margie and Jason looked after them. They wanted for nothing.

Things were going well in the church. Joshua had been able to see the church through growth and service. They had begun another congregation near Marion and Joshua had a young assistant join the ministry.

The girls were growing every day. Emmy and Amanda Belle were becoming quite the young ladies. At fifteen and thirteen they were a great help with the two little girls. Amanda Belle had inherited her mother's musical abilities. Emmy was quiet and withdrawn. She did well in school, but she would rather stay home than go to school. Zoe was stern with her and worked hard at keeping her going. Joshua, on the other hand, coddled Emmy. He gave into her quite often and allowed her to come with him and spend the day at the church.

Zoe always objected and accused Joshua of favoring her too much. Zoe had become "in charge" in a lot of areas of their lives. She had that way about her. It was as though no one else's ideas were right or worth considering, and she made demands on the girls as well as herself. Greth and Jesse were too little to realize how difficult their mother could be, but Emmy certainly felt it.

What does mother want of me? I don't know how to please her. Emmy was thinking as she walked down the sidewalk in front of the church. She was going to choir practice and knew her mother would be expecting her to show up and set an example for the other young ladies. The problem was that none of the other teen aged girls considered Emmy as anyone important. She was a "wall flower," and that was that. Back into her reverie, *I just don't understand why I can't be myself. I don't mind singing in the choir, but I don't want to be the leader.*

As she stepped into the vestibule at the back of the church, she could hear her mother *in that tone of voice that meant, "Look out! Trouble is afoot!"*

"Emmy, it's about time you managed to get here. I would think that the least that you, and others, could do is to be on time!" Yes, Zoe was on a tear today.

"Sorry, Mother, I'm here now," was the best that Emmy could muster.

Joshua was in the back of the church and realized the mood of the day and he cringed at the thought of Zoe's attack, especially embarrassing Emmy in front of the other young people. *I must find a way, Lord, to help Emmy to help herself – especially if we are all to survive.* Joshua offered up a silent prayer.

~ ~ ~

The very next Sunday Joshua was prepared to exegete the passage from Philippians chapter four beginning with verse three that tells us to think on things that are good, pure, excellent and worthy of praise, and Preacher Casey continued as he explained the scriptures,

". . . and if we will do that . . . the God of Peace will be with us. Now, that is the promise of His Word. God tells us, through the writers of His Word, what to do in order to receive God's peace. Jesus speaks of that peace – the peace that passes understanding. The problem is we just don't understand it. That's why it's called 'the peace that passes understanding.' God is good - where God is – and we need to choose to join God where he is – there is peace. In spite of ourselves, our surroundings, our circumstances, our past, present or future. God is good and God is peace. Our part is to think on things that are of God – things that are good, pure, excellent and worthy of praise."

He glanced over at Zoe. She was sitting on the front row with Greth and Jesse. She was looking right at him. She had a strange look on her face. He nodded at her and went on.

"This passage tells us that when we do not do the things that we have learned and know to do – we struggle in all that we do. In other words we try to make it on our own. It will not work. We are made in God's image, the *Imago Dei*. But, we are not God! We never will be God, we wouldn't want to be God if we could. Why, then, do we struggle so as God's children to become God. That is ordering others around, as if we have the right – making judgment calls on others behavior, just because it does not match what we thought one should do or be and most assuredly causing unhappiness and unrest in others when we should be helping them find their peace."

Joshua was reaching out into territory that he thought about much of the time, but hardly ever preached on it. He looked at the expressions of the congregation and he thought they were rather stark. It seemed they were listening, but they looked as though they didn't quite get it. Nothing new in preaching – most times – most people do not get "it." They don't understand what they need to discover.

The sermon ended with the regular invitation to discipleship. The choir led in the singing, the benediction was pronounced and the last amen was spoken.

Emmy and Amanda Belle had managed to be among the first ones out the door. They hoped to escape their mother's eye and ire. She usually had something to criticize about the service, or the people, or their father's sermon or something. They had skipped around to the side of the church where the young people usually congregated after church. It was a large crowd today. A new family had moved to town and had visited church that morning. The girls were discussing the daughter who was their age and the boys were discussing her too. There was an older son, that is beyond the school age teens, he was probably in his early twenties and the girls had noticed him, but dismissed him at the same time.

Emmy had noticed him and hadn't dismissed him. He seemed to be shy and she immediately related to him. The family was just exiting the church and were conversing with her father. The pleasantries and cordial remarks were flying back and forth and Emmy saw the young man scan the crowd as she stepped around the corner toward the front of the church. She caught his eye and he smiled at her. She blushed a heavy shade of scarlet and looked down at the ground. Emmy did not usually attract anyone's attention, much less a pleasant looking young man's attention.

Home for Sunday dinner was next. The Caseys had managed to get someone to help in their home. They had been in Marion going on fourteen years and the church had been generous and encouraging. They had never had a worker and a scholar like Joshua Casey. It was quite ironic that Joshua's first church fired him before he started – and his second church, which really was his first attempt at ministry in the church – was fraught to let him go. They had been able to convince the Superintendent and the Bishop that they needed to keep Dr. Reverend Joshua Casey. There was no argument that the church had grown in the past fourteen years and was an example in the Conference toward supporting missions. Marion M.E. Church was a leader.

~ *42* ~

*"Make allowances for each other's faults, and
forgive anyone who offends you. Remember, the
Lord forgave you, so you must forgive others."*
Colossians 3:33

School was out for the summer and the first month had
come and gone. It was nearing the Fourth of July and
the handbills had gone up all over town that there was to be
a Chataquah. Traveling Chatauquahs were first introduced
in the 1870's there were 21 such troupes operating on 93
circuits, reaching a phenomenal 35 million people a year.

The local newspaper had been advertising its coming for
over a month with headlines like, "The Chautauqua Is the
Most American Thing in America." Everyone was excited
about it, especially the young people. Emmy and Amanda
Belle had been talking it up at home every chance they got
and had convinced their mother that they should go. Zoe
agreed providing that they would take Greth and Jesse with
them. She figured that would cramp their style and they
would have to behave like young ladies.

"Oh, Mother, why do we have to drag them along,"
Amanda Belle didn't hesitate to let her feeling be known any-

time and anyplace. Although Zoe seemed to allow Amanda Belle to express herself, it always made Emmy nervous.

"It's okay, Amanda," Emmy chimed in. She was afraid if their mother got mad she wouldn't them go at all.

"Well, girls, you can either take them with you, or you can stay at home. It makes no difference to me. Take your choice!" Zoe had spoken.

"See, I told you," Emmy whispered to Amanda. "Stop asking her. I'll watch them. You don't have to."

And, so off they went on a Saturday about mid-morning. It all seemed so innocent. The little girls were more excited about the "treats for eating" than anything else. They walked up and down the aisles of the carnival features. They ate, and they strolled. Friends were there and some of them were dragging their little brothers and sisters too. It seemed to be a trade-off for everyone. The food wasn't particularly that good, but it was abundant. Jesse liked the caramel corn and she had managed to down two boxes of it.

The girls took turns, well actually, Amanda Belle took most of the turns walking around with friends. It was a grand event. One could feel so grown-up and independent. Emmy sat with the little girls and even wondered if they should be eating all of what their mother would call "unhealthy" food. By the time they got home the little girls were one, big sticky mess.

It was bedtime the second day after the Chataquah foray. Jesse began to complain with the stomach ache. Zoe knew she needed a good stiff dose of Dr. Caldwell's Syrup of Pepsin and she figured that would do the trick. It didn't. The next day and the next day, with now castor oil, Jesse was vomiting and of course her tummy was puffed up and tender.

Zoe took Jesse to see Dr. Huckaby and he hummed and hawed as he pressed here and there and said, "Looks like we have a problem here, Mother," speaking to Zoe. "What has she been eating?"

"Well, nothing much but a little broth for the last two days, but she probably over ate when the girls took her and Greth to the Chataquah last Saturday."

"And, she hasn't had any relief since then?" Dr. Huckaby frowned as he turned and looked at Zoe.

"No, not at all. I've given her Syrup of Pepsin and Castor Oil – I don't know what else to do. She seems to have a lot of pain in her tummy and she seems to have a fever."

"Well, Zoe, she has more than that. I'm afraid Miss Jesse has an obstruction in her bowels and there isn't a whole lot we can do about it, but wait and hope and pray that something resolves itself and she begins to eliminate this matter."

"What do you mean, Doctor? There isn't a whole lot we can do about it? What does that mean . . . surely you don't mean . . ." Zoe was raising her voice and getting into her indignant mode of *don't tell me there isn't anything that can be done.*

Before she could say another word, Dr. Huckaby – pressed his finger to his lips to *sshhh* Zoe and motioned for her to wait.

"Let's get you all put back together here, Miss Jesse. Here, Mother, you can do that better than I can. We'll take our time here and figure this out." Dr. Huckaby was always so very kind with the little people. He wasn't as gentle all the time. But, he also knew that Jesse was in a lot of trouble and it would take more than he could do to help her.

Zoe was dumbfounded. Surely the doctor wasn't giving up on Jesse. She had been fine less than a week ago. Her mind was racing. She couldn't stop it. She went through the motions of redressing Jesse. She asked Dr. Huckaby what exactly was going on.

Doctor Huckaby was now out of earshot of Jesse, "Zoe, Jesse has locked bowels. We don't know what causes it, but when all of these symptoms are presented no bowel sounds, no elimination, fever, pain, bloating - "locked bowels" is the conclusion. We can't remove enough waste to do any good although I will certainly try that. I would let her soak in warm water, not hot, she has a fever, but tepid water. Her body needs moisture. Is she drinking any liquids at all?"

"No, not since yesterday - she keeps telling me she's going to "frow up.""

"Well, give her a teaspoon of liquid at a time and massage her belly gently if she will let you. I'll come by before bedtime tonight and see if we can help her. Take her home, keep her quiet and pray, Zoe, pray."

Joshua met Zoe and Jesse at the door. Zoe was carrying her and crying as she came in the house. "Zoe, Emmy told me you took Jesse to Dr. Huckaby's. What's going on?"

"I'll tell you in a minute. Let me get Jesse undressed and into bed. She needs to rest."

With that pronouncement, Zoe hurried to the back of house calling over her shoulder for Emmy to come and help her.

In the little girls' room, Zoe turned on Emmy and almost shouted in her face. "What did you feed this child last Saturday at the Chataquah show? What, Emmy? What did she eat?"

"Well, mother, I'm not sure. We were all eating. We had popcorn and corn on the cob and dill pickles and some sausage on a stick . . . I don't know."

"You don't know! You don't know!!!" Zoe was screaming at Emmy by now. Greth who had been in the room playing with her dolls on the other side of the bed – stood up with tears running down her face, "Mommy, Mommy, why are you yelling at Emmy? What's wrong?"

"Go find your father, Greth. Get out of here. We have business to attend to."

By this time Jesse was crying too. Emmy was wasted and Zoe was raging on.

Joshua entered the girls' room and took Zoe by the arm and wheeled her around, "Zoe, for goodness sake. What are you screaming about - or I should ask at whom are you screaming?"

"Don't hold on to me, Joshua, I need to scream and I need to yell and find out what Emmy did to make Jesse so sick."

"Emmy didn't make Jesse sick. Zoe what's the matter with you?"

Speaking to Emmy, Joshua told her, "Emmy, please see to Jesse. I need to take your mother to the kitchen. With that taken care of, Joshua half dragged Zoe toward the door and she twisted and broke away from him. She rushed ahead of him and slammed the door in his face.

"I'm sorry, Emmy. I'm sorry. Please don't cry – just be brave and take care of Jesse. I'll be right back."

Joshua came down the hall and Zoe rushed out of the kitchen to meet him. "This is it – this is it – Your Righteousness – God is doing it again – Jesse is dying!"

"Zoe, control yourself. You don't know that. What is going on?"

"Doctor Huckaby said that Jesse has locked bowels and he can't do anything about it. What do you think that means? For, God's sake, Joshua, what does it take to convince you that our child is dying?"

"Zoe, you don't know that. You're scaring the children. You're attacking Emmy. You don't know what you're doing. You need to calm down. I'll get the doctor for you. We are not going to have this behavior."

"Oh, really! You decide how everyone is supposed to behave. I don't think so, Mr. Godman. I am not going to stand by and lose another one of my children. I need to get to the bottom of this and do something about it."

"We will get to the bottom of it, Zoe, and we will take care of OUR children, but we are not going to have you acting like a mad woman in the meantime."

With that little speech, Joshua left the kitchen to go and see about Jesse and to comfort Emmy. He encountered Amanda Belle as he went down the hall.

She asked, "Father, what is all the commotion about? I just got home and Greth is sitting out on the front porch crying. She said something about Mother being mad at her."

"Well, Honey, your mother is upset. She's just very worried about Jesse. She had been to the doctor's with her and he is concerned about Jesse's condition. I'm going to see if I can help Emmy with Jesse. Will you please go take care of Greth?"

Joshua entered the bedroom and saw that Emmy had managed to comfort Jesse and was sitting in a chair at the bedside. Jesse was crying silently. She looked so pitiful.

"Here, here, Jesse, what's Daddy's big girl crying about? Do you hurt some place?"

"Yes, Daddy, my tummy hurts. Mommie took me to the doctor's and he said I was purty sick."

"I believe you are pretty sick, Jesse, but we'll see how we can make you better. Emmy, you go and help Amanda Belle with Greth. They're out on the front porch. I'm going to sit here with my brave little soldier and see if we can get calmed down."

"Father, I am so sorry. I don't know why Mother is so angry. I am so sorry . . . "

"That's okay, Emmy, you haven't done anything wrong. Just go out and help your sisters."

~ ~ ~

Evening came and went as the girls moved around through the house. Zoe had left the house after her encounter with Joshua. She had just come back and put some food on the table. She called the girls to come to the table and then excused herself to see about Jesse. Joshua had managed to rock Jesse to sleep. As Zoe came in the room, he motioned to her to be quiet. She sat down on the bed and stared at her hands. She looked pathetic. Her appearance was that of a woman many years beyond her age. She had been crying, her face was flushed and her countenance was so downcast that Joshua felt sorry for her.

He got up gently and laid Jesse down in the bed. Zoe moved around to make room and helped pull down the covers to get Jesse settled. Zoe then turned to Joshua and moved into his embrace. She laid her head on Joshua's chest and quietly sobbed. Joshua knew what she was feeling. He was feeling it too. You never forget, nor do you every get used to that horrible realization when you're facing such a helpless situation. If there was only something that you could do? Some way you could make things right and relieve your child's suffering.

Zoe whispered to Joshua to tell him what Doctor Huckaby had said. Jesse was very sick and there was nothing that could be done. It would take a miracle to help her.

Joshua was praying in his spirit as he stood by the bed, holding Zoe. He was praying that God would intervene with a miracle and help his dear little girl.

No help came. Jesse wakened within the hour. She was in extreme pain. Her fever was raging. Zoe sat and held her for hours trying to quiet her and – it was just too much for her little system. Doctor Huckaby stopped by, as he had promised. He examined Jesse again, only slightly this time. He knew the signs. Her system was toxic – there had been too much strain on her heart, she couldn't survive it. He stayed for over an hour and the three adults just sat in the silence.

Jesse died early in the morning, just before sunup. Zoe was holding her as she convulsed for the last time. It was a sad and horrible death. Joshua took her lifeless body and laid her in the bed. At daylight, he went to get help.

Mrs. Huckaby came with the doctor. Someone needed to be with the girls while Joshua and Dr. Huckaby helped Zoe.

~ 43 ~

"God lifted me out of the pit of despair, out of the
mud and the mire. He set my feet on solid ground
and steadied me as I walked along."
Psalm 40:2

Margie and Jason, Emma and Byron were there by the end of day following the horror of the night of death. What to say? What to do? Actually, to be present was all that they could do. When Zoe saw her mother come through the front door, she ran into her arms and let herself go. Her sobs were deep and yet soft. She had been in this place before and while she knew she would survive, at that moment she didn't care if she did.

"Grandmother, I'm so glad you are here," Emmy cried as she came and laid her head on Margie's back, placing her arms around her grandmother and her mother.

Amanda Belle stood apart from them and waited to be recognized. She was grieving in her own way. Somewhat aloof and independent, she did not express her grief. She just waited. Greth was the one that was lost. She was too little to understand. She knew that Jesse was gone, but she was so worried about her mother. Only if she could make it all right for Zoe, would she feel whole again or comforted.

Joshua stepped forward to embrace his father and turned to see Greth waiting to be noticed and included in the sad, sad scene. He reached out and took her hand and held it to let her know she was a part of them all.

The little casket was placed in the parlor that night and church folks began to come to pay their condolences. Zoe was not forthcoming. Joshua made their excuses. People understood. Margie kept the girls with her. Jason stood by with Joshua and Emma and Byron. The four of them intercepted and greeted most of the people. The funeral was the next day. A sad, lonely time for them all. Jesse Vanell had been a happy, vibrant little girl only a week ago and now she was gone. Gone to be with the Lord, that should be comforting yet it was devastating. How do you tell your children farewell?

Joshua's associate pastor, Carl Stanley, conducted the service. The church was filled with mourners. Zoe didn't come. Again, Margie, Jason, Emma and Byron stood by holding the girls and each other together. Mrs. Huckaby stayed with Zoe. Zoe wasn't in tears. She was just "nothing." She didn't talk to anybody. She just sat in the rocker in Jesse and Greth's room and twisted her hankie. She stared straight ahead and breathed in shallow breaths as though it was such an effort, you wondered if she would keep breathing.

Emmy and Amanda Belle clung to each other. They had talked for hours during that long day of the burial. Amanda Belle's strength and resolve was way beyond her years. She was Emmy's salvation. Together they were able to get through those two days. Greth was a loner. Joshua tried to comfort her, but he needed to be comforted himself. It had happened so quickly.

It was so final in so little time.

The older Caseys stayed for almost a week. Emma and Byron returned to Indianapolis on Saturday following the funeral. Their family was growing by leaps and bounds. They had a lot going on in their lives and Emma was expecting. Pastor Carl Stanley had talked with the girls before and after the dreadful days following Jesse's death. Emmy was particularly attracted to Carl and the same could be said for him. Her heart had been challenged. Amanda Belle was her practical, "let's get on it with self." In fact a great deal of what Amanda Belle thought or did was about herself. Greth was the one who was suffering. She was lost without Jesse, actually she was lost without her mother. Zoe was just not present. She was going through the motions of everyday life, but she was definitely not engaged with the needs and emotions of the Joshua or the girls, especially Greth.

Greth suffered through every day. Every attempt she made to draw close to her mother was futile. At six years old a little person is barely old enough to realize the meaning of death, but certainly not old enough to compensate or be compensated unless the adults in their lives reach out to them. Zoe wasn't reaching out to anyone.

~ *44* ~

*"You will keep in perfect peace all who trust in
you, all whose thoughts are fixed on you!*
Isaiah 26:3

Joshua was worried about the girls and especially Greth.
He tried in vain to reach Zoe. That wasn't to be. But,
Emmy was gaining some much needed confidence and at
sixteen she was feeling the normal attraction to the opposite
sex. That would be Carl Stanley. Carl was only twenty-two
and he was open to Emmy's attentions. He was a quiet young
man a very deep thinker . . . the two of them spent most of
their time together talking about life and faith. It was good
for both of them.

It didn't go unnoticed. Joshua was pleased, at least one
member of his family seemed to be coping. Amanda Belle
always coped. You either "coped" with her or you were
ignored. She had her sights set for going away to the American
Academy where Uncle Byron and Aunt Emma were.
Joshua had talked to Emma about it and it looked as though
that would be happening soon.

That just left Greth. That was the biggest dilemma. From
early morning until bedtime she tried to engage her mother
in conversation. She was ready, willing and able to become

the focus of Zoe's attention as the child who was devoted to her. Zoe was hardened. That was her coping mechanism.

It's interesting that in "coping mechanisms" people take different tacks to survive. The two most common attitudes are "control" and/or "crustiness." That is bravado. People who live in the crusty emotion seem to be saying, *I'm just fine. I don't need any help. Why are you worrying about me. In other words, leave me alone.* That was Zoe. Just leave her alone. She would go through the days' activities . . . alone and aloof . . . no time for love or attention that was so needed by Greth.

Joshua recognized what was happening and made extra effort to help Greth. She was taking piano lessons, not from her mother, but from one of Zoe's students who was branching out in the community to teach music. Greth loved that. It seemed to be an outlet for her that satisfied some of her longing and loneliness.

She had friends her age, but they were still little girls in their behavior and thoughts. They hadn't lost their dear, dear baby sister, and their mothers were still "mothering."

What would become of Greth? How would she cope with her mother's indifference to her? Emmy and Amanda Belle were old enough to seek other people and ways of living, but Greth was at that vulnerable age. She blamed herself for everything.

Journey through five generation of
women in the series
<u>**The Daughters**</u>

These are faith-filled stories of women
Living and loving in joy and sorrow.
Their experiences, based on reality, are captivating.
Enjoy as a group or an individual-read.
Allow the summary section of
soul-searching questions, based on Scripture,
to guide you or your group.

EMMA (1812-1857)
Emma, parentless at five, survives through financial panic,
devastating illness and losses of loved ones.
(Published Fall of 2010)
(Available at www.pastorsue.com)

MARGARET (1837-1907)
Margaret, Emma's only daughter, widowed and forced
to remarry in order to provide for her three children.
Zoe, Margaret's youngest, forms personality traits
that will affect lives that follow.
(Published Spring of 2011)
(Available at www.pastorsue.com)

ZOE (1858 – 1942)
Faces tragic losses with an unyielding and
strong personality which changes the
future dynamics of the family.
(Published December of 2011)
(Available at www.pastorsue.com)

GRETH (1890– 1980)
Affected by her mother, Greth, endures life at its
poorest and finds faith at its strongest.
(Available Spring of 2012)

CASSIE (1930 - ??)
Spoiled and abandoned yet answers God's
call to ministry and service.
Faith becomes the key to her survival.
(Available Fall of 2012)

INDIVIDUAL OR GROUP
DISCUSSION QUESTIONS

You might want to do six sessions based on the story line
and the way the characters of the book responded. You
would use six to eight chapters for each session, depending
on how much the group is reading each week.

An individual would also benefit from personal reflection
using the questions and scriptures as guidelines.

Chapter 1: Talk or think about what "you have been given"
and what you are doing with it.

Chapter 2: Where was God when you experienced what
was going on in the Casey family? Can you
give thanks for the good that did come from a
bad experience?

Chapter 3: What does it mean to you to "fear the Lord?"
The word fear can be translated as Respect.
Respect the Lord – talk or think about what it
means to "respect" the Lord.

Chapter 4: Proverbs 20:7 "The godly walk with integrity;
blessed are their children who follow them."
What does it mean to be godly? We are made
in God's image – what does that mean to you?

Chapter 5: Margie has been seriously injured. Talk or think about the consequences of what Others have done? What could Margie have done that would have been better than rushing off half-cocked?

Chapter 6: Do you believe as Deuteronomy 33:27 tells us that "The eternal God is your refuge and his everlasting arms are under you." Talk or think about the fact that God is never surprised by anything.

Chapter 7: Did you expect Joshua to have a turn of heart and become a believer in the Lord Jesus Christ? Talk or think about the quote from Isaiah 26:3 – "You will keep in perfect peace all who trust in you, all whose thoughts are fixed on you." How do we keep our thoughts fixed on Him?

Chapter 8: What do you think it means to "Make thankfulness your sacrifice to God?" How do we sacrifice? How can thankfulness be a sacrifice? The rest of Psalm 50:14-15 tells us "Then call on me when you are in trouble, and I will rescue you, and you will give me glory."

Chapter 9: You've been introduced to Alvina, a faithful and humble daughter and servant of God. Psalm 34 is teaching and calling again: "Come my children, listen to me: I will teach you the fear (respect of the LORD). . ." Alvina has been obedient and faithful and her inner beauty has attracted Jeremy. Had Alvina listened to her father (Father)?

Chapter 10: How do you manage to "live" in the midst of others decisions and actions? Do you put your "trust" in the Lord? Renee was going to have to deal with George's decision. Think about when you had to live with someone else's decision. Did you recognize God's presence in your decision or the outcome?

Chapter 11: "The love of the LORD remains forever with those who fear (respect) him. His salvation extends to the children's children of those who are faithful to his covenant, of those who obey his commandments." (Psalm 103:17-18) This is a generational blessing. Do you recognize that in your family? If not why not – what has happened in the family history? How do we overcome generational problems?

Chapter 12: "Take courage as you fulfill your duties, and may the LORD be with those who do what is right." (2 Chronicles 19:11) How hard is it to allow others to do what is right? How do you deal with the realities of life? How can you better handle those times?

Chapter 13: How are men (women) without excuse? What are God's invisible qualities that we do not take to heart? What or Whom are you able to keep? (Answer: Those or that which you are willing to let go.)

Chapter 14: Recall a time of reunion that was one of the best of your life. What make that time so special? Can something like that happen again? What would it take to make it happen? Do you believe that according to the Word of God "All things work together for good to those who love the Lord and are called according to his purposes." (I Thessalonians 2:18)

Chapter 15: Talk or think about George and Martin going west to (1) help the soldiers, the settlers, the Native Americans? (2) How does that compare to the needs of today that are close to your life either in relationship or community. Proverbs

28:27 "Whoever gives to the poor will lack nothing, but those who close their eyes to poverty will be cursed."

Chapter 16: Talk or think about a time when your heart was light and loving. How do you feel about Jeremy and Alvina having met? Do you think God had a hand in it?

Chapter 17: How are "the everlasting arms of God under" us and ours? Do you have folks in your family that are deployed? What about the families of friends? What do you feel called to do to support them?

Chapter 18: "Do not despise these small beginnings, for the LORD rejoices to see the work begin." (Zechariah 4:10) When have you had a small beginning? How did God show up? What would you advise or encourage someone in small beginnings?

Chapter 19: How important is the directive of God written in Deuteronomy 15:11? "Therefore I command you to be open handed toward your brothers and toward the poor and needy in your land."

Chapter 20: What do you need to "go back to" in order to find peace? What does a godly way look like for you?

Chapter 21: When is the last time you needed to "hold up?" Renee was doing well after learning of George's injuries. What qualities do you think Renee possessed to give her strength to hold up?

Chapter 22: Carol Sue shared her life story about losing her father and then her mother from a broken heart. How can you relate as the Scripture quote tells us "And we know he lives in us because the Spirit he gave us lives in us." I John 3:24.

think she had enjoyed much love? Maybe she didn't know how to receive love?

Chapter 31: Do you think Joshua, Jason and Rev. Robertson handled the Mt. Pisgah dilemma well? Do you think churches can make such judgments? How should the innocent react?

Chapter 32: "Choose a good reputation over great riches; being held in high esteem is better than silver or gold?" (Proverbs 22:1) What do you think of a romantic evening? When have you had one? Would you like to have one again?

Chapter 33: "The LORD is close to the brokenhearted; he rescues those whose spirits are crushed." (Philippians 3:8) Can you imagine how Joshua must have felt? He had prepared over the last five to ten years of his life to answer his "call" to the church. Did God rescue him? Have you ever been rescued by the Lord?

Chapter 34: Dr. Harrall and Emma had a great deal in common. Think and talk about that. (some was good; some was not). Do you think they were a good match? Why?

Chapter 35: Isn't it wonderful to have family and community together to celebrate life? When have you experienced that? What was going on?

Chapter 36: Native Americans were misunderstood and mistreated. How do you feel about that? What if anything can be done even today? Or do you disagree? Based on what?

Chapter 37: Joshua and Zoe's first child didn't have an opportunity to "become older." How close have you been in a situation where a child is lost to death? Do you know about King David's prayers and begging for God to save his son? When he learned his son was dead, what did he do? (Answer: He washed his face, ate and went back to his duties.) How hard would that be? What are we called to do to help those who have such losses?

Chapter 38: This Scripture was a reference in the New Testament. It is one of the jewels of God's Word. "The LORD is close to the brokenhearted; he rescues those whose spirits are crushed." (Psalm 34:18) Joshua had lost the goodwill and confidence of the church people he was to serve and now he has lost a son. How much sorrow can anyone expect in a life time?

Chapter 39: "The Lord gives power to the weak and strength to the powerless." Talk or think about this. Do we realize the generosity of God's care and grace? Do we believe that God really does this? Can you give an example?

Chapter 40: "Let your roots grow down into him, and let your lives be built on him." (Colossians 2:7a) Can you imagine – what good came out of the "bad/wrong" done by the "church?" Can you think of a time when the good overcame the bad?

Chapter 41: Time has advanced and Zoe seems to be the worse for wear. Can you think of why? Especially why do you think Zoe treats Emmy like she does? And, why does she not disturb Amanda Belle? The Scripture from Hebrews 2:1 says "We must listen very carefully to the truth we have heard, or we may drift away from it." Do you think Zoe ever knew the truth? Or do you think she has drifted away? And, why?

Chapter 42: The Colossians 3:33 scripture calls us to "allow for each other's faults, and to forgive anyone who offends you." Have you ever known anyone who was so willing to blame someone else in a tragedy? Can you account for Zoe's harsh attitude toward Emmy? Sorrow and heartbreak does strange things in the absence of the Lord's presence in your life.

Chapter 43: Joshua was truly upheld by God's strong arm as he was lifted far enough out of the pit of despair and was steadied as he walked through what had to be done. What would be your counsel to someone acting like Zoe was? How or what can we do in a situation like that?

Chapter 44: How hard for a parent to make up for the "lack of love and caring" for a child they hold in common. Greth would be forever changed by her mother's boycotting attitude toward her. In the next book you will learn of how Greth survived . . .

CPSIA information can be obtained at www.ICGtesting.com
Printed in the USA
LVOW092046151211

259564LV00001B/1/P